BECCA REDFORD
& THE BIG BAD
WOLFHOUND

SHAWNA ROMKEY

BECCA REDFORD AND THE BIG BAD WOLFHOUND
Copyright © 2017 by Shawna Romkey
ALL RIGHTS RESERVED

Print ISBN: 978-0-9939958-9-7
eBook ISBN: 978-1-7752478-0-7

Cover Art: Dark Imaginarium Art & Design
Editor: Lindsey Loucks, Midnight Library Editing Services
Interior Formatting: Author E.M.S.

Published in the United States of America.

Detention, homework, werewolf slaying...what's your Monday look like?

All Becca Redford wants is to survive her parents' divorce and get through high school with as few detentions as possible, but her family legacy gets in the way.

All Ben Hunt wants is to maintain his clean cut, varsity football image, but he has a secret to keep.

They'll need to find a way to be together without Becca and her wolfhound killing Ben, and the werewolf wars bringing about the end of slayers and hunters all together.

To everyone who has ever loved and lost a dog,
for you have known true love and true loss.

And to those who have ever rescued a dog. You're the real
heroes.

Chapter 1

Becca

Sigh. Detention on the last day of school. Who does this? I mean who schedules this? Apparently I do this. I do detention regularly, but the last day? Come on! I should've skipped, though that's how I got here to start with.

Thirty more minutes of detention. Of this school. Then off to Grandma's house we go. Then a new school, but I can't think of that now.

I glance around the room at the few other losers in detention. Jesus Howard Jones, if this is my last day, why didn't I skip? Who cares? What will they do? Make me come back from my other school to this one for a detention in the fall? Screw this noise.

I stand up and gather my empty backpack.

"Miss Redford?" Mrs. Marx, the detention teacher, says.

"Yeah, I'm done," I say, taking a step to the door.

"Withhold your transcripts."

"Huh?"

"What are they gonna do, you're wondering. What are

they going to do if you leave the last detention of the school year? They'll withhold your transcripts."

I don't know how important that is, but it sounds important. I look at the other three troublemakers in the room who all have eyes on me, waiting to see if I lead the revolt.

I don't feel like leading a revolution today, but I don't feel like being bested by a middle-aged chem teacher, either.

"So?"

"So, you won't graduate, you won't go to college, you won't get a job, and your life will be ruined." She smirks at me and pushes her bifocals up her nose.

That seems important, but I won't graduate for a few more years anyway. Still, it seems like a lot of responsibility for a lousy thirty minutes.

"Fine," I say and drop my things on the floor dramatically before plopping back down in my seat.

The losers all put their heads back down, staring at their desks.

God, school is stupid. I have nothing better to do though.

After detention, I'll head to Grandma's to unpack the rest of my things. My mom left my dad and has been slowly moving us to Grandma's to stay until she can "get on her feet." So that's something to look forward to, moving out of my home with my dad, leaving my school. Ha, well, I hate this shit hole, so I can't pretend I care that much. We haven't lived here that long, just a few years. But I can use the fact they move me around so much when I need to make Mom feel guilty about something. Still, I'm not happy about leaving my dad. She may not love him anymore, but I do. I don't have a choice.

2

Sitting here seems to be the better option of the two: moving out or staying in detention.

I don't even have that many friends I'll miss. I didn't do much here, just went to class occasionally and went home. I'm no honor roll student, cheerleader, or newspaper reporter. I actually liked being at home with my parents.

The corner of my eye starts to sting, so I wipe it and look out the window. It wasn't about me, they said over and over. Duh. It was about them. I know that. It extremely was not, absolutely was not, monumentally was not about me. If it was, they'd stay together, because if it was up to me, they would. I'm insignificant, as per usual. It was totally about them. I just tag along. I am nothing. I am nobody. If it was about me, they would've asked what I wanted to do. They couldn't have waited it out two more years until I was off at college or working at a circus full-time or something somewhere, anywhere? Nope.

But alas, such is my life. Maybe something fun will happen at my new school. Maybe they won't have detentions on the last day of the year. Maybe they won't suck so bad that I skip to stay home and listen to music. But with my luck, it will suck, too.

The bell finally rings, after I've worked myself into a state, and I reenact my previous attempt at leaving, though successfully this time. I consider saying something rude, but Mrs. Marx wasn't the one who gave me the detention in the first place, so why bother? I consider shouting at this school to go screw itself as I leave the front doors, but it's not worth it.

The hallways and parking lot are cleared out. Everyone else already celebrated the last day of school an hour ago because they didn't have detention. I hate awkward goodbyes anyway. If anyone cares, they can find me on the face that is book, though I rarely post anything there either. And besides, I don't feel like celebrating even though it does mean I have three months off.

I yank on the door of my blue Honda Civic a few times to get it to open—it always sticks—then throw my shit in the passenger seat. I roll down the windows manually—no power windows and locks here. The Civvy is hardcore. As I leave the parking lot of Shittydale High School, I give it the middle finger salute and speed away.

Wow, I'm cool.

Grandma's house is only an hour or so in the country, depending on your fondness for speeding. It'll be quieter than my old place and good to spend time with Grandma, I guess. It's nice. It's by the lake, so not a bad place to live for the summer. Not a lot else going on around there though. It's a pretty small town. There's a convenience store and a community center on the lake where you can rent canoes.

I hope she has decent Wi-Fi. God, I hope she has *any* Wi-Fi. Fear grips my heart.

I said goodbye to Dad this morning, but driving away hits me harder than I thought. "Don't worry about things you can't change," he always told me. I can't change this, I guess. I could beg and plead, but I can tell this was harder for them than it was for me. I leave it to them to make the adult choices. I'll deal with the fallout.

I turn on the radio loud, let the warm air blow through the open window, and whip my hair around like I'm in a Kansas tornado. I don't care. Maybe the music will blast the hurt away while my wild hair hides my face from any oncoming traffic.

When I pull into Grandma's gravel drive, I realize how small her house is. It's a tiny cottage with a stone fireplace on the side and rust-colored shutters. She has daffodils planted in the front that are in full bloom, and peony bushes on the side. She's on a large lot on the water, with a sloped yard leading down the back to an old dock. Behind the house is a small barn where she keeps her dogs. She's a bit of a dog nut. I hadn't heard anything about dogs lately, but she has a million of these giant gray dogs she breeds and apparently sells the puppies for big money. That is what pays her bills, she says.

I used to love playing with the dogs in the back when I was little, and I remember they dwarfed me, but we haven't visited as much lately. I wonder if they'll feel small to me now.

Mom's car is already in front. The trunk is open. I park behind her.

The sounds of deep barks greet me as the back screen door opens and my grandma comes out flanked by two ginormous dogs who nearly knock her down, rushing past her on their way to me.

I stop and cross my arms over my chest, my feet planted, the way Grandma taught me to as a child, to keep them from knocking me down or thinking I'm threatening. They are still huge. My growing hasn't made them seem any smaller. Their heads hit me around waist height.

"Lugh, Meriden, sit!" They calm their attack. "Becca dear! So glad to see you! How are you?" She approaches, her arms outstretched, and the tone she uses seems to relax the dogs.

These two are new to me. They sit on their haunches in front of me and turn to licking instead of charging with teeth bared. I slowly unfold my arms and hold my hands palm up to them to let them get my scent. They nudge me and almost knock me over, when Grandma gets to me and embraces me in a big squeeze.

"I'm good, Grandma," I lie. "Where are the other two?" I struggle to remember their names.

"Brigid and Lir?" She pulls back and purses her lips. "They passed away a few years ago. Wolfhounds don't have a long lifespan, unfortunately." She glances at the other two and pets their heads fondly. "These two are from their line."

Way to go, me, for being such a downer. "They're nice dogs," I say. I couldn't think of anything better.

She looks at me. "I'm glad to see you, though the circumstances... Well, you know."

"Yeah." I will not start crying. Instead, I plaster on a fake smile mask. "I'll get the rest of my stuff." I turn to my car.

"Yes, yes. Your mom has most of it inside. She's taken the other bedroom downstairs, so you can have the one up."

"Great." I slink my backpack over one shoulder and get a box out of my trunk.

When I enter, I'm hit with the smell of Grandma's house. Baking bread, flowers, and potpourri most likely, but it's always hard to pin it down. Bread isn't actually baking. It's as though the scent has permeated the crocheted blankets, ruffled curtains, and other fabrics throughout the house, so that it will inevitably hold the scent forever. I smile as memories waft over me with the smells, then the grandfather clock plays the song I only hear at Grandma's and chimes five times.

I hear mom rustling around in the back bedroom and shout, "Hey, Mom."

"Honey!" she shouts in answer, then the sound of glass shattering follows. "Shit."

"Nice to see you, too. I'm heading upstairs," and I do as I say.

"I'll be up in a minute. Shit." That's my mom.

The two gray brindle dogs race me up the stairs, almost killing me. "Yes, doggies. Hi. Thanks. Now move your asses." They jostle me to the only room upstairs where I plunk the box down.

This room is probably the largest in the house and has its own bathroom next to it, but I guess Grandma prefers to stay downstairs, and Mom probably felt guilty about moving me, so she gave me the good room. Who knows? I'll take it. It's big with slanted ceilings and a window in the back overlooking the lake, which I immediately take advantage of. I'll have a nice view this summer anyway. Lots of trees are in the back, but they don't block my view. I can see all the way down to the dock and a few houses across the lake. It's a beautiful day, which is why I see some people in canoes in the back already.

The view is nice. Maybe it'll keep my mind off my life. That's the mission. Stay occupied. Enjoy the time with my grandma. Enjoy the lake. Don't be sad.

I set the box down by the bed and unpack. Again. In another new place. Same shit, different day.

The area looks pretty quiet, really. I hope it's not too boring living here. I doubt anything much goes on though. I mean, I'm living at my grandmother's house. What could happen?

CHAPTER 2

Becca

I unload the rest of my car and start setting up in my room. It has bare bones for furniture: a queen bed, a dresser with a mirror over it, a chest of drawers. But it also has a small walk-in closet. With some posters and my computer table, this place will be all set. I open the window and inhale the smell of the woods and the water.

"Supper!" Grandma calls from downstairs.

When I get down, I see that she and Mom have made my favorite.

"Tacos? And it's not even Tuesday," I say, grinning.

"Your mother said you liked them," Grandma answers. One of the dogs nudges her as she brings the plate of shells to the table. "Lugh! Oh wait, it's his dinner time, too. Don't wait for me," she tells us as she heads out back with her two helpers at her side.

Mom smiles sadly at me. What's the point of a sad smile? Either smile or be sad, but the sad smile doesn't cover anything. It doesn't fake anyone out. You aren't fooling anyone. I sad-smile back.

"How was your last day?" she asks.

"It was the last day." I start filling a taco shell with the good stuff.

"Was it hard for you?" She sits across from me at the table and passes me the lettuce.

I shrug. "No harder than the last three." It's a bit of a jab. My parents, even when together, weren't the definition of stable. We moved around a lot. Today was my last day at my sixth school.

"That's good, I guess," she says and takes a drink of beer.

"Where's mine?" I ask.

"It's five years from now." She smiles and probably thinks she's funny. It's cute how she thinks I haven't had beer before.

"Right. Five."

"Becca!"

"Sure, I'll wait. Just like you did."

"Touché. Mom says there's a girl your age who goes to Park High just down the street," Mom tells me.

"Awesome."

"Well, you can try," she says.

I can try? Did she really just say that? Isn't me being here trying? And really, why bother? I may only be here a year or two. Why make friends when it makes my leaving them harder? That's my theory. That's why I don't have friends. That's what I tell myself anyway.

"I'll try, Mom," I lie.

God knows who this girl is. Grandma has always tried to get me to play with her friends' grandkids my whole life. Just because I was five and this other girl was five doesn't mean we'll be insta-friends. The same goes for this new high school girl. She could be a total bitch or a total nerd or a total loser or a total stoner. Just because we'll end up at the same school doesn't mean we'll be friends. I keep all of this to myself.

Plus, friends are overrated, really. I do okay on my own. I can pick the music and the movie and the TV show. I don't have to wait for people to show up. I don't have to listen to their problems.

Grandma comes back in, out of breath, the screen door in the kitchen slamming shut behind her. "Lord have mercy. Those dogs'll be the death of me. You have to check out this litter, Becca—"

"Mom," my mother says with a cautioning tone.

"Well, she is living here now, Jessica. She's bound to see them at some point."

What is this about? Mom is staring daggers at Grandma.

"What?" I ask.

Mom ignores me and keeps glaring at Grandma. "I told you, Mom, that Becca has no interest in the dogs."

"They're puppies for God's sake, Jessica. Everyone has interest in puppies." Grandma smiles innocently at Mom.

I shrug. "I like puppies all right." I really don't care about puppies so much, but feel like Grandma needs defending for some weird reason.

Mom breaks eye contact with Grandma and turns back to her beer. "Becca doesn't want to be saddled with taking care of your dogs, Mom."

There's something to Mom's tone. It seems pleasant all of a sudden. Victorious even. I'm suspicious.

"You know damn good and well that's not what I'm trying to do," Grandma snaps, and I don't think I've ever heard her swear.

"I can help with the dogs," I offer. I don't have anything else to do.

"See?" Grandma says. "After dinner, we'll go have a look—"

"Mother!" Mom says, and her dagger tone is back. "I told you I didn't want her to have anything to do with your...damn dogs!"

"We're just going to look at the dogs, Jessica. It doesn't mean anything." Grandma's voice softens. "It most likely doesn't mean anything," she says slower, more pointedly.

Mom chugs her beer and stares at her phone, clearly done with this conversation.

"Tacos are good," I say with my mouth partially full.

Grandma smiles at me and holds the glance a few seconds longer than normal before turning back to her dinner.

After dinner, I offer to clean up. Mom abandons her three empties and storms to her room. Awesome way to end the day, Mom.

"I'll go talk to her," Grandma says, and I finish up the rest.

I can hear their raised voices from Mom's room. Then they quiet and whisper. I turn the faucet on and let it run while I tiptoe to the hallway to listen.

"You moved her here," Grandma says.

"I didn't have a choice."

"That's bullshit, Jessica, and you know it. You moved her here. Somehow, someway, you wanted this for her."

"Never! Where else was I supposed to go?

"You could've stayed with Ryan for one thing."

"Oh, thanks for your support, Mom."

"Jessica, there are a million other places to be in this world with your daughter. You chose here. Maybe the stars aligned, maybe the fates collided, but for whatever reason, destiny, bad luck, whatever, here you are. You can't hide from it now."

"After everything with Ryan, and now this?" Mom breaks into sobs.

I tiptoe back to the kitchen and wash the dishes, looking out the window over the sink at the barn. What the hell did any of that mean? Wanted what for me? What stars and fate and destiny? Or bad luck? What did any of it mean, and why on earth were the dogs the trigger of Mom's outburst in the first place?

I dry the dishes, try to figure out where they go, and brush it off to Mom having three Coronas and zero tacos for dinner.

CHAPTER 3

"So what do you make of all of this with your parents?" Grandma asks me as she puts the skillet away.

I shrug. "Does it matter?"

"Of course it matters."

"They do what they need to do. I don't want them to get divorced, but what I want plays no part in it." I sit back down at the table.

Grandma puts two bowls on the table, then grins conspiratorially. "I have ice cream!"

"Ice cream makes everything better!" I say. "Except diabetes."

"Well, we don't have that, so it will all be better." She spoons three scoops into my bowl and passes me a spoon. "What you want does matter, Becca."

I shrug again.

"I think what you mean is that it doesn't change your situation," she adds.

"True. I mean, I know they love me and care about me,

but you're right. What I want won't affect them. I know they want me to be happy, but this isn't it. But if they got back together because of me and were miserable, then I'd feel bad." I'm talking too much. I spoon a big bite of ice cream into my mouth to shut myself up.

"But you still have to get through this however you can."

I nod and keep eating.

She stops looking at me and semi-changes the subject. "The lake will be good for that. Fresh air, cool water, nature, the woods. All of it has always been good for my soul. And there's a girl down the road...Madeline? Madison? Something like that. Works at Lake Pizza. She's real nice. I can invite her family over for a BBQ if you want."

"Thanks, Gran. I'm good. I'll be okay. I don't want you to worry about me." I tell her the truth. I'm sure she's worried about Mom. I'll adapt, like I always have before.

"Well, they have dances at the high school a few times in the summer. Just community events. You could go to some, meet some people—"

"Sure, sounds good." I'm back to lying again. It sounds horrible. Maybe back during the sock hop when Grandma was my age it would be fun, but yikes. Hard pass.

The truth is, I don't like doing anything. I don't like dances or people or the outdoors or school or sports or art or science or or or. I just don't care about any of it. I don't get attached to places. I don't get attached to people, except my family, and look how that's turning out. I like to shop sometimes. I like to play video games sometimes. I like listening to music, but I'm not really into anything.

My parents always hated that. They wanted me to try soccer and piano lessons or this or that. I just don't care.

Whatever. When I was little, I'd do my homework and try to avoid the teacher's wrath, but after junior high, I didn't care about that anymore either. School didn't matter because I didn't know what I wanted to do when I grew up. Getting detention didn't matter because it didn't keep me from doing something else I'd rather be doing.

They even took me to therapy for a while, but the therapist said, "You can't make her want to do stuff or like stuff. She'll find something eventually."

I haven't.

See, the truth is, if you don't care about anything, you can't get hurt. You can't get disappointed. You can't lose something important to you.

Grandma gathers the dishes. Lugh or Meriden or whichever dog it is yawns, and it sounds more like a big squeak than a yawn. I frown.

"Silly dog," she says to it. "Speaking of"—she shoots a look toward the hall and lowers her voice—"want to go see the pups?"

"Sure." I absolutely couldn't fucking care less.

She leads me to the barn-style shed and turns on the light inside. It has two levels. The bottom is set up in what looks to be six tiny horse stalls. Each one is filled with straw and is open, except for the one closest to the door. I look down inside to see eight little brindle puppies sleeping next to their mother.

Grandma smiles. "The puppies." She keeps her voice hushed so as not to wake them, I guess.

"They're cute," I whisper.

"They are. Just four weeks old now. They'll be ready to go in a few more weeks."

"You must hate to sell them."

"I do, but I don't. And I don't always sell them. I keep

the best of the litters. Lugh and Meriden. Rhiannon." She motions to the one with the puppies. "Angus is around here somewhere and Morrigan."

"They just hang around here?"

"Wolfhounds are pretty territorial. They may run off every now and then, but they don't seem to bother anyone on the lake. A lot of the houses are vacation homes and remain empty, and their owners know me and are happy to have the dogs on patrol."

"They're nice. And you've been doing this a while, right?"

"Our family has been doing this a while, yes." She smiles at me like she's amused at my ignorance. She flicks the light off and heads out, shutting the door.

It's then I notice the doggy door that leads inside. It's large enough for a pony to get through. I guess it has to be.

"So that's it?" I ask.

"You didn't like them?"

"No, they're fine. I just mean, that's what Mom was concerned about?" Maybe this separation thing has her overly emotional.

"Well..."

A deep snarl sounds from the darkness of the woods. Grandma holds up a hand to stop me. The snarl flares and erupts into a fierce growl. My heart quickens, and I scan the trees to see where it's coming from, but it's too dark to see anything, except two eyes that glint when the light from the house hits them just right.

"One of yours?" I ask quietly.

I wait for her to call out one of those Irish names she'd mentioned to me. I wait for her to yell at it. I wait for her to do anything, but she stands frozen, her hand still up to me.

The growl quiets down to snarls again, and from the

trees leaps a huge gray blur, lunging straight toward me. I freeze where I stand, and all I see are yellow eyes, open jaws, and bared white teeth coming my way.

If my life hadn't been so boring, it would probably flash before my eyes.

I'm going to die.

Why is my grandmother just standing there?

The two claws hit me right in the chest and knock me to the ground. *Oooof.* The air escapes my lungs, and I brace for my throat to be ripped out. As quickly as I was hit, the thing with the claws and teeth over me gets knocked off with a huge force of impact. Low snarls and growls sound beside me, and I turn to my right to see one of Grandma's dogs facing off with a wolf.

In one leap, the wolfhound puts the wolf in a headlock with one paw and clamps its jaws down on the wolf's throat. The wolf yelps and falls limp, and the dog stops and looks at me. I'm still frozen on the ground, afraid to move or speak. It bounds over and sniffs my face and my neck. It nudges my head, and I realize I haven't breathed yet. I cough desperately to get air. And it licks me and whimpers.

I think I may have wet myself.

I catch my breath and gently push the dog away.

"Are you okay?" Grandma asks, rushing over.

I nod. The wolfhound sits in front of me now, panting through its fierce fangs, and wags its tail.

I push myself up to standing and dust off my jeans. Grandma raises both hands to her mouth, and her eyes seem to be filling with tears.

"What the f—" I say, but stop before I cuss. "Is that a freakin' wolf?"

She laughs and wipes tears away.

"Why are you crying?" I ask.

I catch a shadow by the kitchen door out of the corner of my eye and see Mom turning away and walking inside. What the...

CHAPTER 4

"What the hell is going on?" I demand. "I mean, what the eff?"

"Come inside, dear."

"But what about that thing?" I point at the wolf.

"It's a wolf, Becca. You're in the country now."

"Whatever. And that!" I point at Morrigan. "It was like a demon of death coming at the wolf!"

"She's not an it. She's a she," Grandma explains. "And it's funny you should think that. Morrigan is an Irish name. She's a goddess of battle, fate, and death."

"Gran!"

"Oh, you're fine. Come inside, and I'll try to explain." She heads inside like nothing's wrong.

I glance at the dog who sits patiently beside me. When I make eye contact, she meets my glance, and her tail taps a few times at the attention.

"And what about this?" I say, jutting my chin in the dog's direction.

"Come inside," Grandma says, holding the door for me.

I take a few steps to the back door, and Morrigan stands and follows. I stop and she stops. I take a few steps again, and Morrigan mirrors me.

I shake my head. "Whatever."

I go inside, and the slight tapping of the dog's nails on the tile floor follows me. Grandma shuts the door behind the dog.

"You're letting her in? She just murdered a wolf." I hold my hands up to Grandma, like what the hell.

"She's fine. You will never be safer with another living thing. Now sit down," she says.

"Are you mental?" I'm seriously losing my cool. "I'm sorry, Gran, but really. Were you not paying attention? That was a dog fight from hell. Are you sure you're okay to be out here with these dogs?"

Mom sighs heavily behind me. "Sit down, Becca. There's something we need to talk to you about."

I have no response to these two. They're acting weird, and I had a near-death experience with a wolf and a dog who they think should now come inside like it's a freaking hamster.

"You've already had the talk with me, Mom. I know all about the birds and the bees. Oh yes, and then you had the other talk with me already about how you and Dad are getting a divorce. Then there was the talk about how we were moving. Again. I think I'm all talked out." I say all that, but I sit at the kitchen table anyway.

The dog plants itself right next to me and stares. At me. I try to ignore it.

Mom gives Grandma a look, raising her brows. "See? Don't you think she's had to deal with enough?"

"Granted, your marital troubles could have had better timing, but that can't be helped," Grandma says.

Mom rolls her eyes and turns away in the kitchen archway.

"Tea, dear?" Grandma asks me.

"No. Thanks."

"Jess?"

"I'll make some coffee," Mom says and busies herself while Grandma takes a seat next to me.

She takes a deep breath. "You may not know a lot about our family, but my father came to the States from Ireland. Our family has bred Irish wolfhounds for as far back as I've traced our genealogy. We've bred and sold them, and we've trained them. We've kept them as pets and companions." She says all this while looking at me, watching me. The same way the dog keeps looking at me.

"Okay. And?"

Morrigan wags her tail whenever I speak. I frown and give it the same look I give to the captain of the football team at my last school who asked me to homecoming. Go. Away.

"And wolfhounds are special dogs. They were originally bred to fight the wolves in Ireland, hence the name wolfhound. They're big and their fighting style leads to taking down wolves."

"Gran, what does this have to do with anything?"

"Just tell her," my mom says.

Grandma smiles. "You're a wolf slayer."

"I'm a wolf slayer," I repeat to make sure I'm hearing this correctly. I look to Mom, waiting for her to explain to me how Grandma has dementia, and we're taking her to a home tomorrow, but Mom pours herself a cup of coffee and leans against the counter.

"In a nutshell," Grandma continues. "My maiden name is Connolly. You belong to the Connolly Clan of wolf slayers."

Grandma gives a quick side look to Mom, but I don't know what that means. I don't know what any of this means.

"For centuries we've bred and trained wolfhounds to fight the wolves. Most of our wolfhounds are regular dogs. I breed them and sell them to earn my living. People buy them as house pets because they are unique and look regal. They are the dogs of nobility. But some of our wolfhounds are special." She reaches over and pets Morrigan who wags her tail. "They choose a person they want to train with. They choose someone to bond with, and I think Morrigan appears to have chosen you."

"But I don't know anything about training dogs or slaying wolves. This is ridiculous." I'm thinking I don't want to be known as the dog girl.

"Most of us don't know it at first, but we pass the knowledge down to those who are chosen. I hadn't a clue when I was chosen. But you have me. I'm here to train you to be a slayer and to train your hound."

I blink. I look at Mom who sips her coffee. I blink again. "This is nuts. I don't want to train dogs or kill wolves. And this dog could've killed me! How is that choosing me?"

"She didn't attack you. She jumped at the wolf. She was protecting you. And she hasn't taken her eyes off you since."

That's true and seriously unnerving. "That means she chose me to train her?"

"Usually, a dog will attach itself to its slayer in that way. Watching them, staying at their side, looking up at them adoringly. You may have noticed, Lugh chose me." She cocks her head in Lugh's direction, who I realize is rarely out of Grandma's sight.

I glance at Morrigan who again taps her tail a few times. "But I don't want to train a dog."

"Well, then that's a waste. These dogs are rare. It's rare to have one that is special. Even more rare to have one choose its trainer."

"Too bad. Find another dog trainer."

My mother sighs. "In our family, it's a great honor to be chosen to be a slayer. Only those with a special inner strength can do it. The dogs are said to sense that. It takes extreme mental acumen as well as physical abilities you probably don't even know you have. If you are chosen, it means this is your destiny. You can fight it, and you can avoid it, but you will be altering your fate."

I shake my head. Now Mom is adding to this bizarre conversation. "Mom, you're talking crazy."

"Your mother should have prepared you for this better," Grandma interjects with a sharp look at Mom. "This conversation shouldn't be such a shock to you, and I'm sorry for that. I was chosen when I was your age. Your mother…"

Mom turns away to the sink.

"Your mother should have talked to you about this."

"The clan is dying out," Mom says. "I didn't think…"

"The clan is not dying out. I have dogs on this very property who have the blood of Culain in them. Morrigan is of Culain's line! You only hope we're dying out."

Mom slams her cup down on the counter. "Yes, you're right. I hoped the clan was dying out, so my daughter wouldn't be saddled with this craziness!"

Grandma stands up and crosses the kitchen to stand

toe-to-toe with my mom. "You prefer to saddle her with your own craziness, your own problems!"

"Mom, Gran." I rise and move to get between them. None of this is making any sense. I put my hands up to part the two of them, and Mom whacks my hand away.

In a flash, Morrigan is in front of me, teeth bared and snarling at my mom.

"Morrigan!" Grandma chastises, but Morrigan doesn't settle.

Mom raises her hands up in surrender and steps back, but Morrigan is still in front of me ready for battle.

"Talk to her, Becca. Calm your dog," Grandma says.

"Morrigan, it's okay," is all I say, and Morrigan looks up at me and sits, wagging her tail. I have to admit, that's kind of cool.

"Great," Mom says.

"I didn't choose your daughter," Grandma says to Mom. "And I didn't bring her here."

"I know. I kept her away as long as I could. I tried to keep her from this," Mom says.

"Why? I mean, it's just a dog. I'm here this summer. I didn't have aspirations of being a dog trainer extraordinaire or wolf slayer or anything, but I can work with Morrigan over the summer. I don't have anything else to do." I don't want to train a dog to be honest, but I don't want this drama between my mom and my grandma. Mom's been through enough lately.

Mom shakes her head. "Oh honey, you don't understand the dangers."

I laugh. "Of being a wolf slayer? It'll be like hunting or something, right?"

Gran and Mom exchange a knowing glance. "Honey, I may have sugarcoated it a bit," Gran says to me. "Irish wolfhounds are wolf slayers, but the special ones, like Morrigan here, don't only kill wolves."

Creepy. I frown. "Okay...what else do they kill?"

Grandma looks to Mom who nods. "Honey, they kill werewolves."

CHAPTER 5

Becca

"Werewolves?" I burst out laughing. "Okay, then. Well, let me just get my silver bullets and some garlic," I mock and pat my pockets for supplies. "Or is garlic for vampires? Oh well, no big, I'll kill some vampires, too, while I'm at it. Does that work for you, doggy?" I ask Morrigan, who tries to lick me and wags her tail some more. "Awesome, let's go!" I feign walking out. "Seriously, you two, where's the hidden camera? Clearly I'm being punked."

But it's odd. Mom and Grandma have never been big on practical jokes or any jokes whatsoever. It's out of character for them to pull some big thing on me like this. Especially today, on this day, the day I move out of my family home with my two parents, the day I leave yet another school. If they are joking, it's a cruel joke to play today.

Grandma puts a hand on my shoulder. "Becca, I'm sorry, but it's not a joke. Let me show you," she says, and gestures toward the living room. "I should've started with this, but I didn't think you'd be chosen so soon. I wasn't thinking."

I pull away. "You know what? I'm good. It's been a long day, and not necessarily a good day. I need some air." Before they can stop me, I'm out the kitchen door and down the cement steps to the backyard. I walk around to the front of the house, ignoring their calls to me. I need to walk. I was cooped up in school all day, then detention, then the car ride, then unpacking. I really do need the air and the exercise. Maybe I'm imagining all this. Maybe it's just a dream.

Wolves and werewolves. How ridiculous! I'd swear Grandma was losing it, but Mom? Maybe she'd had a sympathetic breakdown. I'd heard of different kinds of mental illnesses where people feed off each other so that it's almost contagious. Maybe with Mom and Dad's problems, Mom coming here and being close to Grandma, who is literally off her rocker—maybe they are contaminating each other.

My mind races as I walk briskly down the paved road in the dark. The moon gives some illumination through the trees as I go. I head in a straight line so as not to get lost. Crap, I don't have my phone, and getting lost when I'm on a dramatic walk would be embarrassing.

Then I hear the panting at my side. Morrigan slipped out with me and trots at my side. Awesome.

"What are you doing here?" I ask her.

She keeps trotting beside me, eyes on the forest on both sides of us.

"You seem perfectly harmless now."

She lopes happily along.

Like Grandma's two dogs do with her. I frown. Like the two she had before always did when I visited as a little kid. Could those have been her were-wolfhounds? No. It's nuts. I noticed I'm whistling a tune to myself. I can't quite place it.

How is this happening? How could they do this to me? I miss Dad and start wondering where he is and wondering if I should call him. Would that upset Mom? What kind of relationship am I supposed to have with him now? Are they going to fight over me? Will she be jealous when I talk to him or visit him? How often am I going to get to do that? I don't want two Christmases.

My mind goes off on a tangent, a realistic tangent about things I should be thinking about. About reality. Maybe Mom and Grandma are just trying to distract me from my crappy life. *Who's afraid of the big, bad wolf?* The words to the tune come to me.

Morrigan barks loudly behind me.

"Look out!"

I don't even notice the changes around me until someone rams into me, charging full speed, and tackles me to the ground. This is getting to be a habit of mine, getting body slammed and having the wind knocked out of me. I open my mouth to protest when the loud roar of a pickup's engine rushes past where I was just standing.

"Are you okay?" he asks. It's a he. He pushes himself up on his elbow.

"Ummm, no, not really." Oh, he means because I was almost roadkill.

He stands and holds out a hand to me. I take it. It's really warm. Feels good. Then the snarls come from behind me.

"Oh God," he says, looking at Morrigan.

"It's okay, Morrigan," I say and she calms.

"Oh, it's with you?" he asks, eyes not leaving the dog.

BECCA REDFORD AND THE BIG BAD WOLFHOUND

"Unfortunately."

"Look, I'm sorry about that, but that truck was barreling down the road—"

"You don't have to apologize for saving me." I finally look at him. It's dark, but he looks about my age and potentially cute.

"Well, I didn't have to knock you to the ground. I was just on the other side of the road and didn't want to see you get hit. I'm Ben, by the way. Ben Hunt." He holds out his hand.

I shake it. "Becca Redford."

"You're not a tourist," he says and looks at Morrigan. "I mean, I don't know you, and the lake area is pretty much a small town, so I know everyone around here. I don't know you, but I do know those dogs." He gestures to Morrigan. "You must be staying with Helen...errr...Mrs. Russell."

"She's my grandmother." I dust off my jeans and become suddenly conscious of how I must look after a day of driving and unpacking and getting knocked down multiple times. I reach up to tuck my hair behind my ear, then realize I had my hair up on the top of my head, so it wouldn't be in my way while I unpacked. I can feel half of it hanging down in loose strands around my face. I must look like a crazy person. That would be appropriate, though, because I feel like a crazy person.

He looks like a typical high school guy: clean cut, T-shirt, jeans, some muscles. I realize I must be staring.

"Are you here for a visit?" he asks.

"Yeah. No, no, I'm here for a while, I guess. The summer, at least," I stutter.

"That's good, then. I'll see you around. I live in the house across the lake from your grandmother's."

"Oh, nice."

Morrigan positions herself between us, and though she's no longer growling, she's staring at Ben pretty intently.

He notices, too, and takes a step back. "I've seen your grandmother's dogs before. Scary."

"Sometimes."

"Do you want me to walk you home? I was just at the pizza place with the guys." He points in the direction I was heading. "But I can take you back home if you want. You shouldn't be out here at night by yourself." He looks behind me into the trees.

I laugh. "Really? Why?"

"Oh, nothing, just speeding drunk idiots in big pickup trucks." He smiles.

"I think I can manage, but thanks," I say. Though I couldn't manage mere minutes ago. I would've been killed if left to my own devices. "I don't want your pizza to get cold."

"I'm not really thinking about my pizza right now," he says. He stares at me a second, then shakes his head and backs off that comment. "Okay, well be careful. There's not a lot of traffic out here, but you still can't walk in the road."

"Okay, thanks." I'm a total idiot. "Enjoy your pizza, Ben Hunt."

"Will do." He smiles again, and it's kinda radiant. "Enjoy your walk, Becca Redford." He turns, looks both ways, jogs across the street, and heads back into the pizza joint that I hadn't even noticed I'd been approaching.

"Well, that was embarrassing and amazing," I say to Morrigan, who watches Ben until he's inside, then looks at me and wags her tail.

LAKE PIZZA, the sign says. PIZZA – BEER – SNACKS – GROCERIES. Hmm, an all-in-one kinda place. I see him at a booth in the window with two other guys, then hope he can't see me standing there staring after him.

Wait, how had he gotten across the street and pushed me out of the way of the truck so fast? It wasn't far, but still. He would have had to see the truck speeding, me walking like a dork in traffic, and run into the street to get me.

I shrug. "Let's go, Morrigan," I say, and we head back to Grandma's.

Maybe it won't be so bad here. I mean a pizza place within walking distance and all. Then there's Ben. It's stupid. I don't know Ben. I know it was dark, but he seemed kinda cute, and he's apparently the rescuing type, which means he's nice and a good guy and cares about other people. And he has friends he eats pizza with. I guess that's all I know about him, but so far, it's a good start.

And what does he know about me? I'm the dog girl who lives with my grandmother, wanders aimlessly in the street, and looks like Cinderella after a long day of cleaning out fireplaces. Ugh. Terrific.

A few times on the way back, Morrigan freezes, eyes on the forest, and then runs off through the woods. Both times she returns to my side, not begging for pets or trying to lick me, but looking to the woods like she's on patrol. Must be her breed...or her special werewolf slaying skills. Eye roll.

"Do you see some werewolves?" I ask her in my doggy-talk voice.

She doesn't wag her tail, but keeps her eyes on the trees. She apparently doesn't like my mocking her abilities.

"Whatever, dog. You're as nuts as they are."

I enter Grandma's through the front door, Morrigan

tailing me. Grandma and my mom are in the living room on the couch. They both look up at me, worry tainting their eyes. A large book that looks like an old scrapbook rests on the coffee table in front of them.

"Where were you?" Mom starts in.

"Out." I keep walking to the stairs to head up to my room.

"Becca, honey, wait," Grandma says.

"It's been a long day." I don't stop moving. "I'm going to bed."

"Let her go," Mom says. "She gets like this sometimes."

I roll my eyes. Yeah, Mom, well sometimes my life is being ripped apart. And sometimes my family is mental. So yeah, sometimes I get like this.

Morrigan bounds up the stairs behind me.

"Where do you think you're going?"

Grandma peeks around from the bottom of the stairs. "She'll probably want to sleep with you."

I can tell Grandma wants to explain more of this magical werewolf mystery whatever to me, but she holds back.

I stand aside and let Morrigan come into my room before I close the two of us in. My bed is the only part of my room completely ready for use, thank God. I dig through a trash bag full of clothes until I find something comfy enough to sleep in—a T-shirt and boys' flannel boxer shorts that I get Mom to buy for me for just this purpose.

Morrigan sits patiently and watches me get changed. I wonder if she needs water or anything. I've never had a dog before. Mom always seemed kinda anti-dog, now that I think about it. I rummage through my duffel bag to find my bathroom stuff and head across the hall to my very own private bathroom. I could get used to this part.

I shout down from the top of the stairs. "Is she going to need food or water or anything?"

"I'll be up," Gran says.

I get ready for bed and unpack some of my stuff. I take my birth control pill. It's not that I have all the sex and have to avoid getting pregnant. I started taking it to regulate my periods, and taking it reduces my periods to one every three or four months, which is a total bonus.

I return to my room, and Grandma has put a bowl of water on the floor and laid out a flannel blanket at the foot of the bed for Morrigan.

"She should be fine," she says.

"Okay."

Grandma sits there like she wants to talk, and I most definitely do not want to, so I act like she's not there, plug my phone in to charge by the side of my bed, turn on the lamp on my nightstand, and pull down my quilt.

"Becca."

"Don't."

"We will need to talk about this more. I'm just so sorry… I'm so sorry about how it's happening and what you're already going through. I should be more sensitive—"

"Why? I'm fine." I finally make eye contact with her.

"You will be," she says.

What the hell does that mean?

"I'll let you get some sleep. Do you need anything else in here?" She stands in my doorway.

"I think I'm good." I climb into bed.

Morrigan, instead of lying on her newly placed flannel blanket on the floor, jumps in bed with me.

Grandma purses her lips. "I thought that might happen. I can take her out if you want me to. She'll complain, but…"

Though she's ginormous, Morrigan lies at my feet, and it's a queen bed, so there's room for both of us. I hate to admit it, even if it's just to myself, but it's kind of nice actually.

"She's okay."

"Good night, sweetie.

"Night."

She turns out the light and closes the door behind her. I sigh. I want to talk, but I don't want to talk. I want to sleep, but I don't. The day's events rush through my mind. I sit up and turn around. A window overlooking the lake is right behind the head of my bed. I look out to the opposite side.

He lives across the lake from us, he said. I see a few different houses on the other side of the lake with lights on. I try to guess which one is his, then slide down under the covers and turn my lamp off.

Ben Hunt.

Morrigan rests her chin on my feet. Cute.

CHAPTER 6

Ben

"What was that all about?" my older brother asks as I come in the front door.

I watch Becca with my peripheral vision as I return to our booth and respond to them. "I don't really know."

I smile and my brothers say something else, but I'm preoccupied. I see her standing at the side of the road looking on for a minute before she shakes her head and turns back the way she'd come to her grandmother's. I have a clear shot of the road that the LaRette boys ripped down, and had seen her walking along, paying attention to nothing.

"It was a girl," Sam teases, then follows up with a punch to my arm.

"It was," I admit. "Teddy LaRette was speeding down the road. Nearly hit her."

Both of my older brothers turn to eye the road where it happened.

"So...you had to run out and save her?" Nic asks.

"Well, yeah."

"You idiot," Sam says, laughing and shaking his head.

"What? Like I'm gonna sit here and watch some girl get run over?

"Don't you think she might have noticed your super speed?" Nic asks, his voice hushed. Nic, being my older brother, speaks with more diplomacy than Sam.

"She didn't say anything. I don't think she saw. She was in her own world."

"Dumbass," Sam says again. He lifts a slice of meat lovers' and chows down.

Nic turns and looks down the road. She's disappeared from sight. "Anyone could have seen you."

I scan the pizza joint. No one is giving us strange looks. "No one gives a crap about anyone but themselves. You know that.

Nic exhales deeply. "I know. Just be careful."

I take a slice of pizza and focus my attention on it when I add, "That may be kind of difficult."

Nic furrows his brows at me. "What do you mean?"

I'm thinking about how gorgeous and mussed up she looked. I'm thinking about how she needed me to help her. I'm thinking about how she smelled of vanilla and lilacs.

I raise my eyes to meet his. "She's a Connolly."

CHAPTER 7

Ben

"I'm sorry, she's a what now?" Nic asks.

Sam stops chewing and stares at me.

"She's a Connolly. I don't know if she's in the clan or anything, but she's Helen Russell's granddaughter. She's staying at the house for the summer." I blather on, hoping to get their eyes off me.

"Stay away from that," Sam says with his mouth full, then goes back to working on his pizza.

"I have to say I agree," Nic adds.

I can't stay away from *that*. She's my age, she lives right across the lake from me, she's interesting, she's pretty...

"Okay." I take a bite of pizza.

"I mean it, Benny," Nic says. I hate when he calls me that. "That leads to nothing but trouble."

"All girls do, according to Dad."

"Well, Dad's right this time. Don't get involved. Leave her be, and she'll be gone at the end of summer," Nic says.

"Or she might be going to Park High. I'm not sure. I'm not sure she's sure."

"Dammit, Ben! It's bad enough having Mrs. Russell right across the friggin' lake from us. You're gonna what, go over for tea? Start dating her granddaughter?"

"I don't know! I'm not going to do anything. I knocked her out of the way of LaRette's truck. I might never see her again."

"Might."

"Or I might have classes with her in the fall. I don't know. I'm not planning anything. I'm not running over with a batch of roses to court her or something."

"But you've thought about it!"

"I haven't thought anything! Honestly, I met her like five minutes ago. Can we just drop it?"

"Oh, we'll drop it...for now."

"Good." I try to get back to my pizza and avoid eye contact, but I can feel Nic staring in my direction.

Sam keeps looking back and forth between Nic and me. He's the middle child, so he usually waits to see who to ally with.

"Just because she's Helen Russell's granddaughter and had a dog with her, doesn't mean she's a slayer."

Nic slams his fist down on the table, drawing more attention from the other patrons in the pizza place than I'd like. He looks around and lowers his voice. "She had a wolfhound *with* her?"

Crap. I guess I had yet to mention that part. I shrug and look around the room. Blood rushes to my face. "I don't know."

"You just said she did!" Sam jumps in.

"This changes everything," Nic says. "We have to tell Dad."

"Don't!" I beg my older brother. "He'll send me away."

"Ben! What are we supposed—"

"Nothing! What we've been doing for years. Mrs. Russell has lived across the lake since we moved here. Nothing has happened."

"She has made it clear that we maintain our distance. So no, nothing has happened yet."

"Right. Yet. So why do we have to do something now? Won't that draw attention to us? To me? Nic, come on."

The muscles around Nic's jaw tighten. He looks to Sam, though we both know Sam won't be much help. "Okay, Ben, but I swear to God—"

"It's fine, Nic. I'll make sure it's fine." I hope he believes me. I hope I sound convincing.

We finish our pizza in silence, then head home in Nic's truck. I play video games in my room for the rest of the night, in an attempt to keep the attention off myself, but I have a feeling Nic isn't going to take any of this lightly.

It should be fine. I just have to stay away from Becca and Mrs. Russell's house. Unfortunately, nothing interesting happens at the lake very often. A new girl, my age, with an interesting family, with messy blonde hair, a David Bowie T-shirt, and a rescue-me disposition doesn't walk into my life every day. I can't kick the feeling that she needs me.

I climb into bed and swipe my phone to open my music. I choose my David Bowie collection, put my earbuds in, and listen. I wonder what her favorite Bowie song is. I glance out my window over to the Russell house. The moon reflects off the lake and sends a straight line to her house. Weird.

I wonder if she really likes Bowie or just got the shirt at some shitty, phony mall store because it looked cool.

Probably the latter. She's probably basic like the rest of them. At home, watching *Friends* on Netflix and polishing her nails. Probably doesn't even care she was almost killed tonight. She's probably not thinking of me at all.

Or she's a werewolf slayer. I'm so screwed.

CHAPTER 8

Becca

I wake up with a gasp. Morrigan, still at my feet, jerks her head to attention, ears out to the side. My heart hammers in my chest. I take several deep breaths to slow my pulse. Nightmare. Images of bared fangs and flying fur bounding from the trees, a full moon, howls, and snarls quickly evaporate from my mind as I join the conscious world. I can't remember specifically what the dream was about or what I was doing in it, and the pictures of it fade as I try to grasp at them, like grabbing a reflection in a pool of water. Gone.

I'm sitting up, and the sun is streaming in through my window. I realize where I am, and my breathing and heart rate both go back to normal. Morrigan rests her chin back on my feet.

I'd been restless all night. The day-to-day situations I'm facing racing through my head.

Morrigan lets out a quiet whine and eyes me through her scruffy hair that sprouts all over her face. Her eyes are huge, like she is, and dark brown, and her eyebrows slant outward and down at an angle, making her look kind of sweet and sad all the time. Her nose is big, her feet, her long ass tail. All of her is huge. I swear she must weigh the same as I do, if not more. I lean toward her and pet her back, and she automatically falls to her side to give me a prime shot at rubbing her belly.

I giggle. "Silly girl."

She stretches her front paws out and reaches from one side of the queen bed to the other. She's got to be as long as I am, too. She lets out a long sigh.

"You need to go out?"

She springs up, leaps off the bed, and stands at the door waiting for me. I pluck my phone from its charger and check emails and messages. Dad had texted me "good night, sweets."

I fire off a quick response to him telling him I'd gone to bed early. Then I pad across the braided rug and open the door, releasing Morrigan on the world. She bounds down the stairs sounding like a herd of wildebeests while I make a quick break for my bathroom.

When I get downstairs, the smell of bacon and eggs lures me into the kitchen. I don't say anything. I don't know what to say, but I'm curious as to where Morrigan went to. I look over Grandma's shoulder out the kitchen window to see if I can catch a glimpse of her outside.

"I let her out," Grandma says, smiling.

"What?" I ask, regarding her smirk.

She shakes her head. "Oh, nothing. Are you hungry?"

One thing you can count on Grandma for is food. "I am, but I can't eat like this all the time, Gran. I'll gain a million pounds."

"I won't do it all the time. Just this once," she says, and

I know it's a lie. She puts a plate full of breakfast in front of me at the table, so I sit and eat.

"Where's Mom?" I ask with a full mouth.

"She's up and gone. Showing a house already."

It was convenient that her real estate agency had a branch nearby. She wouldn't have to deal with finding a new job or having a break in work. I, however…

"I should get a job," I say.

She laughs.

"What?" I ask with a bit more hostility than I did the first time.

She shakes her head. "I'm sorry. I shouldn't say anything, but you won't have a lot of time for a job."

"This again?"

She goes over and opens the kitchen door. Morrigan bounds in immediately and lopes over to sit beside me. Her chin is even with the kitchen table. She could use it as a chin rest if she wanted. She sits and stares at me.

"She's not begging, by the way. She's just…looking at you."

"Great. If only all the boys adored me as much as you seem to." Aaaaand I talk to dogs now.

"I'm sure they do, honey. You're beautiful."

"Says my grandmother. Like that's not biased or anything." I take a bite of bacon. "Although, there was a boy last night."

She puts her hands on her hips. "Last night?"

I nod and chew. "Yeah, by the pizza place. Said his name was Ben, and he lives across the lake from us." I jab my fork in the rough direction of where he'd live.

Grandma stands there, hands on hips, spatula in one hand, and I don't see her breathe for a few seconds. "Ben Hunt?" she asks, slowly.

I nod. "Yeah, he's kinda cute. Said he knew you."

She holds her pose. "Well, everyone knows everyone around here. It's a blessing and a curse." She says it with a light tone that seems forced to me.

"So you know him?"

She turns to the skillet and busies herself with more bacon. "Uh-huh, yeah, the Hunts. You've heard of the Hunt family. They're famous in Kansas City. They own damn near the entire Plaza, the sports teams, the amusement parks, a huge shipping company. They are Kansas City royalty."

"Oh yeah? He's one of them? Jackpot!" I say, teasing her.

"Well, not one of them, no."

"I was going to say, the houses around here are nice. They aren't 'I own the Kansas City Chiefs' nice."

"He's a distant relative. Let's see. He lives with his dad and two brothers over there. Nice boys. Always out on the lake. They don't make any trouble." She hasn't turned from the stove since this conversation got moving.

"Okay, well that's good. Is there anything else? You seem bothered by the fact that I met him."

She turns. "Me? No, of course not."

She sits down with her cup of coffee in her hands and looks at me.

"Cool."

"I'm glad you got a look around. You saw Lake Pizza. The gas station is next to it, then the community center, the church, the bank, and the post office. And that's about it for the greater Silver Lake area." She smiles and her wrinkles gather at the corners of her eyes.

I'd never noticed her as being old until now. She's in great shape for a grandma. She's not one of these white-haired, bun-wearing, plump, apron-sporting grandmas.

She used to run marathons, but that was probably ten years ago or so. I think she swims a lot now and hikes with the dogs. She's got some sun on her face and some gray streaks in her shoulder-length bob. Working outdoors with the dogs is good for her. She's healthy, but she is aging.

"It'll be fine, Gran. I can run into the city if I need anything. It's not far. I'll probably do some more exploring today." Maybe I'll run into Ben again. And I'll get out of the crazy house for the day and not have to deal with the topic of—

"We should talk about what I told you last night. Sooner rather than later," she says.

I clean my plate, then tidy up the kitchen. I pour myself a cup of coffee and add three heaping teaspoons of sugar to it from Grandma's little floral-painted china dish on the center of her table. I stir, clinking the spoon to the edges.

Morrigan tilts her head and watches me. Her ears, which normally hang straight down, perk out a bit to the side.

"All righty then, Gran. Let's get this over with. Let's go talk about werewolves." I head into the living room.

I plop down on the couch where Mom had been the night before. The tattered book lies on the coffee table before me. The cover is a deep green with faded gold letters, but I can't make out what they say.

"It's Irish," Grandma says and sits next to me.

Morrigan follows her in and lies down in front of the coffee table.

"Where to begin?" she says.

"How about beginning with the truth," I say.

She takes my hand and eyes me. "Becca, everything I'm telling you is the truth. I wouldn't lie to you or tell you fairy stories. Not ever, but especially not now."

She's freaking me out because I believe her, but I know what she's going to tell me can't possibly be true.

Taking a deep breath, her hands move over the cover of the book. The leather is rough, and she runs her fingers over it. "Wolfhounds are an old breed. They date back before the birth of Christ. Julius Caesar mentions them in his writings. Etchings and engravings of them have indicated that they may have been brought to Ireland as far back as 7000 BC."

I raise my eyebrows and nod. "Impressive." I look over at Morrigan who watches us intently.

"They are more than dogs. They are sight hounds. They see even the slightest movement at great distances, and they'll take off after whatever unusual thing it is at great speed. To take it down at all costs. They are guard dogs. Loyal to the core. They were called wolf dogs at first because they resemble wolves," she says.

"Hmmm, they seem a bit derpier than wolves," I say, looking at Morrigan's tall, awkward body, her dark brown eyes, and her too-big-for-her-face-or-for-anybody's-face, nose.

Grandma looks at me, confused.

"Goofier," I explain.

"Oh, well, sure, when they're just sitting there, but when they fight..." She opens up the book and flips through a few pages toward the end. Each page is full of old black and white photos. She scans them and points. "There."

She shows me a picture of what looks like an old timey fox hunt, but swap little beagle dogs with giant wolfhounds, and swap the cute little fox being cornered for a snarling wolf. The two wolfhounds flanking it look fierce. They are all bared teeth and angry glares.

"Yikes." It was what Morrigan had looked like to me when she jumped at me from the trees multiplied times a hundred. "Okay, definitely not derpy."

"Indeed. In ancient Rome, they were used to fight wolves and lions in the arena. They are not to be trifled with. The ancients called them *Cú Faoil*. They were bred to fight beasts, so they were bred to be large and bred to be strong. During certain periods of Irish history, only nobles were allowed to own them. They are a noble breed trained for a specific purpose.

"My family—*our* family—as you know, is Irish. That's what gives you that red hair—"

"My hair is not red! It's blonde," I argue.

She ignores me and continues. "I have many other photo albums like this one passed down from generations to me. Our family, the Connolly Clan, started breeding these dogs a thousand years ago. The ledgers of the breeding logs are over there." She gestures to a bookshelf I've seen a million times that is full of identical thin, black, hardcover books from top to bottom. I've never pulled one out before. "From the very first pair. Their names, parents, birth weights, litter information, sizes… All of it is saved there."

"Why?" I wander over and pull one out to thumb through. It reads like a biblical entry. *Dec. 25, 1934. Caithne & Dagoth – litter 4 – 5 females, 2 males*, with weights and measurements for each.

"I think it started out as the family business, but also to trace the bloodlines. According to our records, my great, great, great, great, great grandmother"—she looks up and counts the greats on her fingers—"started breeding them because she was allowed access to Culain, a legendary wolfhound at the time who had special abilities."

"Spoiler alert, you already told me this last night, so let me guess. Culain could kill werewolves."

"That's what they said."

I put the ledger back and turn to her. "That's great, Gran. Okay, so our family was cuckoo and thought there were werewolves back in ancient Ireland, so they bred wolfhounds for hundreds of years, and you still have some from that same line from the magic wonder dog, and Morrigan is one of those, I take it?"

"Well, aside from the cuckoo part, yes."

"Okay, well why didn't you just say that? Breeding wolfhounds is important to our family, and Morrigan took a liking to me and bonded, so you want me to start breeding wolfhounds when I'm older? Carry on the family business?"

"Well, no, not really—"

"And that's why Mom was so upset, because she wants me to go on and do super impressive things with my life and be a lawyer or a doctor or a real estate agent or something. It makes sense now." I piece it all together so that it's logical and realistic.

"No, Becca. That's not it. You got most of it correct, but you're missing the important part. There was a werewolf problem in Ireland. That's why they brought the wolfhounds there. Certain warriors trained with them and took them out on hunts. Here." She turns the book around to me and points. "See those two? That's Aiden and Berin Connolly, two brothers who were famous werewolf slayers. They would be your great, great, great uncles. They are the modern slayer trainers. Our family had a slayer in each generation. I was the slayer in my generation, and you…"

I sigh heavily and flop back on the couch next to her.

"But Gran, you're missing a very important point here. Werewolves. Do. Not. Exist."

At that, she flips the book a few pages and stabs her finger at a full-page black and white photo that shows a creature standing on two legs, its front legs outstretched and lunging at someone. The head and the body aren't entirely wolf-like or human-like. It's a freak show hybrid of the two. And the photo is so old, its edges have some sort of fancy curved trim. The entirety of it is yellowed. There's no way it could be Photoshopped.

"Oh honey, that's the point you're missing. They 100 percent do."

CHAPTER 9

Becca

I run through every possible reason that there would be an old photo of some strange creature like this in my grandmother's scrapbook. None of which make sense. Photoshop, weird exposure issue, a mean practical joke, a guy in a wolf suit. None of them play out. Its legs are too skinny to be an actual person in a suit. A person wouldn't fit in it. A stuffed creature? A wax-museum-type creature from a weird carnival?

"Becca, I know it's hard for you to grasp, but stop trying to come up with reasons for this and accept it. It will be much easier for all of us. Just because you don't believe it, doesn't make it untrue." She puts a hand on my knee.

Dumbfounded, I realize my mouth is hanging open. "It just can't be."

"It can. When your mom was little I used to tell her about the werewolves. She grew up knowing about them and hearing stories passed down from generations, almost in the same way that families tell their children stories about Santa Claus or the Easter Bunny, the only difference being that werewolves were real.

"So she knew and was sworn to secrecy not to tell kids at school or anyone because it was our family's responsibility to deal with the monsters, and we didn't want anyone to be afraid because we could handle it," she says.

"Why didn't she ever tell me?" I ask in shock, staring off into nothing.

Grandma exhales heavily. "Well, she didn't want to be a part of it anymore. She said she wanted a normal life for you. She let you come around the wolfhounds but wanted no talk of anything else."

"Has she seen one?" I'm partly asking normal questions out of shock and halfway out of believing and somewhat playing along to try to trip her up.

"She hasn't, but she's seen the aftermath. She wasn't allowed to go on hunts, but she came to investigate sites with me. Sites where livestock or other animals had been mauled. Never sites with human victims."

"So she doesn't know for sure."

"She knows, honey. She's seen the dogs and me after a fight." She pulls her shirt back off her shoulder and shows me some brutal scars in the shape of five deep claw marks. "She knows where this one came from. She knows where all the others came from. And she knows how her father was killed."

"Grandpa was killed by a werewolf?" I can't believe I'm saying these words or any sentence with the word werewolf in it.

She nods.

"And you've seen them?" I ask her.

"More than I'd like to admit," she answers.

"How many have you seen, and how many have you killed?" I kind of expect her to blow it off and not have a real answer.

"I've seen 125 werewolves. I've killed 111."

I open my eyes so wide I feel like they're gonna pop out of my head. My mouth is hanging open again.

"I didn't kill them all without help. Some were part of my training, and some were with other hunters."

"Are there other hunters around?"

She shakes her head. "Not many who hunt like we do. There are still some werewolves and slayers in Europe, but there haven't been many in the Americas. There hasn't been a need for slayers until recently. Maybe it has something to do with my age, or maybe because recently more werewolf sightings have been occurring. That's why it's more important than ever that you accept the calling and train to be a slayer. I'm the last of the Connolly Clan. These dogs are the last of the line of Culain. Once we're gone…"

I don't want to hear what happens once they're gone.

"I'll do it." I say it before I can think it through. I can't bear the worry in her eyes. I can't bear her not knowing what would happen to her dogs once she's gone. I have no choice. She's my Gran.

"You will?" There's hope in her eyes, and relief washes over me. If all I have to do is accept the madness, then I'm in.

"I'll be the slayer." I half expect a beam of light to shine down on me or dramatic music to play, but Gran just hugs me. Morrigan's tail thumps the floor a few times. "I mean, yeah. So…what do I do?"

CHAPTER 10

Training starts today. I get ready and put on a sports bra and yoga pants. Morrigan follows me around everywhere I go. I head to the kitchen and let Morrigan out. I make some toast and chug some OJ.

"Gran?" I call out.

"Yes, dear." She comes around the corner. She's wearing khaki Capri pants and a light, floral-print top. Her hair is back in a red bandana.

"Training. I'm ready!" I say as I stretch my calves.

She frowns at me. "Okay, well," she says, looking around. She opens a drawer in the kitchen and takes out a notebook, which she hands to me, then slaps a pen on top of it.

"What's this?"

"This is training, day one." She smiles.

"What do I do with it?"

"Day one you spend out there." She jabs a finger in the direction of the yard and barn. "You hang out with the dogs, and you write down everything you notice about them."

Now I'm frowning. "I hang out with the dogs and write down journal entries about them?"

She nods. "Yup."

"That's it?"

"Uh-huh."

"All day?"

"All day."

I stand there staring at her, hoping there's more to this than that. She doesn't move or say anything else.

"Well, that sounds boring as hell," I say.

"Oh, and you'll tend to their every need. I'm taking the day off dog duty. You'll feed them, give them fresh water, let them out if necessary, let them back in if they tire of being outside. I'm going to town for a spa day." She heads down the hall to her room.

I shout after her. "I don't know how to take care of dogs! I've never had a dog."

"You'll figure it out," she shouts back to me.

"This journal stuff... It sounds like school! I'm done with school for the summer!"

"You're not done with slayer training school for the summer! You're just starting!"

All day with the dogs. I run upstairs and put a T-shirt on since I'll be outside all day, and go back out to start my observations.

Hours later, I report back to Grandma, who is looking way too relaxed as she reclines all the way back on the lounger in her yard. She's wearing her sunglasses and a wide-brimmed gardening hat. She fans herself with an Oriental fan.

"I'm done," I announce.

She doesn't open her eyes or turn to acknowledge me.

"And?"

"It's boring as hell," I say, curbing the actual swear that came to mind.

"What did you learn?"

I shrug, though she can't see it as she is refusing to come out of her post spa-day bliss. "I don't know."

She sighs heavily. "Then guess what training day two looks like."

"What?"

"If you learned nothing—"

"Fine." I pick up the notebook. "I learned that dogs are a pain in the ass and a lot of work."

She chuckles. "True."

"And that they want to eat all the time, and they want to be pet and want to lick you all the time."

"True for wolfhounds anyway. Anything else new?"

"I don't know."

"What are their names? What did the puppies do? Which dogs get along best? Which dogs are alphas? Which dogs do you think are were-wolfhounds? How do they communicate? What motivates them?"

I plop down on the grass next to her lounger. "I don't know all of their names. The puppies played, ate, peed, pooped, and slept. Morrigan is an alpha, for sure, and a were-wolfhound. They communicate by whining or barking. And most of them are motivated by treats."

"Wrong. Try again tomorrow."

"What? That's BS, Grandma! I didn't get all that wrong. I know Morrigan is a were-wolfhound at least."

"It's a pass/fail test. Today you failed."

"Whatever. I don't see what the point of this is! Are you trying to get me to hate the dogs?"

She sits up and turns to me. "Absolutely not, but right now you don't know the dogs. You don't know enough about them to love or hate them. You only know enough to tolerate them.

"You need to know the signs Morrigan sends you. You need to know what she needs. You need to know if she's scared or hurt. You need to be able to take care of her and understand her if you're going to go on hunts with her."

"But what about fighting and learning how to use silver weapons to kill werewolves?"

She laughs to herself. "Honey, you have it all wrong."

"What do you mean? You said I was a werewolf slayer."

She waggles her head side to side and purses her lips. "I did say that, and I can see how it could be misleading."

"How so?"

"You're not the one who does the fighting and killing." She points to Morrigan, who as always is at my side. "She is."

I try again. I remember as many of the questions she asked me as possible, so that I can pass today. I go straight to the barn and head for the puppies. The dogs all wear nametags on their collars, so I take a look at each one and jot those down in my notebook under the heading Dog Names. Rhiannon is with the puppies most of the time, letting them nurse while she sleeps. She's tall enough to occasionally step over the board Gran has blocking the puppies in, so every now and again she takes a break and goes outside for fresh air. I leave the barn door open for ventilation and light.

I scoop out the puppy poo and find fresh hay in the next stall over, and I make sure there is clean water in the half a dozen bowls Gran has set around the inside and outside of the barn.

Rhiannon spends time with Angus when she's outside, and he periodically comes to visit her when she's with the pups. He must be the puppies' father.

Morrigan sticks to me most of the day, watching me as closely as I'm watching her. She seems to be waiting for me to do something, though I don't know what.

Lugh and Meriden stay close to the house and become extremely excited when Grandma comes outside to water her garden or get the mail.

I watch all of them until I think I know the ins and outs of the five adult dogs and the eight puppies. Though I know Morrigan is a were-wolfhound, I start to doubt if she's an alpha. Lugh pushes her around a lot, and when he roughhouses, she runs behind me until he gets bored and leaves. I change my assessment of her and add to my assessment of him.

I try to teach Morrigan to sit, and while she'll take the treat from me, she isn't extremely interested in it. She seems to be motivated by my approval.

"Good dog," I tell her, no matter what she does, and her tail wags. I ruffle her ears and give her some affection, and she leans into me almost like she's giving me a head-butt, but she snuggles the top of her head against my leg, her muzzle under my arm, and huffs to breathe. "Can you breathe, silly?"

She seems not to mind the breathing problems as long

as she's getting her ears scratched and her head is making constant contact with me.

I find an old tennis ball in the barn. "Can you catch, Morri?" I ask, and feign throwing the ball to her.

She stands and her ears perk out to the side. I throw it for real this time, and it bounces off the top of her head. Half a second later she snaps at where the ball had been, but it's long gone. We try this again, several times. She can't catch for shit.

"I thought you were a sight hound. Look," I tell her, and slowly throw it her way.

Again, it passes her, and a half second later she pounces down, splaying her feet out in front of her, and keeping her butt up in the air, trying to play, but missing the ball by more than a mile. I can't help but laugh at her.

We run around the yard a bit. She really likes that. She barks at me a little, not the way she did the first night. These are more like little playful woofs rather than rip-your-throat-out, snarling barks. I chase her, and then she chases me. I'm actually laughing and having fun, when she stops and stares at the lake.

I lean over and catch my breath, my hands on my knees when I see what she's looking at. Two guys are out in a canoe toward the middle of the lake.

Her ears are pinned back against her head now, and she gives a small woof, then a louder one, then goes full-blown-terrifying barking as she tears off to the dock.

"Morri, it's nothing. Come here," I shout after her, but she doesn't respond. I jog down the dock toward her. She's stopped and positioned at the end. "Morri, stop."

Her barks quiet, but her ears are still behind her. The small ridge that runs down her spine is up in a long spike, and her tail juts straight out.

"Morri, it's okay." I wave to the guys in the canoe. "Sorry," I call out to them, not that Morrigan did anything. And I see him.

Life-saving Ben is one of the guys in the canoe fifty feet away from my dock. Great, and here I was running around like an idiot with my dog.

Others had been on the lake today. Someone waterskied by, a few with kayaks paddled past, some kids in tubes were screaming and splashing each other. Morrigan didn't react. This is the second time she's seen Ben, and the second time she's flipped out at him. Is she jealous, maybe? Can she sense something in me like my attraction to him? Or is there something about him she doesn't like?

Chapter 11

Ben

"Well, there's your answer, Benny," Nic says.

I wave at her when she calls out an apology and flash a weak smile. She wasn't supposed to notice us out here. Stupid sight hounds.

"That's not an answer. She's living with a woman who has like twelve dogs. She's out playing in the yard with a dog. Big whoop." I try to convince him, but have I convinced myself?

He turns and looks at me. "Are you kidding? Look at that dog. We've been watching her for what, thirty minutes? Has the dog left her side once?"

"It's probably glad to have someone to play with. Mrs. Russell doesn't run around the yard like that anymore. Can we just go? Our cover is blown now. Just row like we were cruising the lake." I need to get out of here. I don't have a shirt on, and she's looking at me.

Nic rows away, as if it was the plan all along. I give another weak, embarrassed wave. She does the same, and we put some distance between us. The sun is warm on my skin. It's a good day to get the canoe out.

"She's pretty," Nic says.

I frown, though he's in front of me and can't see it. "So?"

"So it's going to be harder than I thought to keep you away from her. I've gotta tell Dad."

"What? Because she's attractive? Like if she were ugly, it'd be no problem to keep me away?" I'm offended on behalf of all girls everywhere.

"Well, since attractive by literal definition means hard to keep away from, probably not," he explains. I can hear the smirk on his face.

"Thanks, bro."

"Am I wrong?"

He's not, so I keep my mouth closed.

"Just don't tell Dad. Can't you manage this yourself? You're twenty-one for God's sake." I dip my oar in the water and row, trying to play to his desire to be in charge.

"I could tell Mom."

"If I thought you could find her or that you were even halfway serious, we'd have some major problems." I'm not amused with him joking about our estranged mother. It's kinda cruel, actually.

"You wanted to do a row-by. You wanted to see if you could get some clues as to what she was doing here. You are the one wanting to spy on her," he says.

"I don't want to spy on her. I just wanted to see if we could get some answers." I'm not being creepy. I hope I'm not being creepy. Am I being creepy?

"I think we got some answers."

"I'm unconvinced," I argue.

"What, you thought we'd see her in the middle of

slaying a werewolf in her backyard this afternoon? What more do you want?" Nic asks.

"More than enjoying the summer afternoon in the backyard with a dog," I answer.

"Fair enough. We'll keep an eye out. Maybe not from an exposed point in the middle of the lake next time," he says.

"If you ask me, we've just set precedence for us doing this all the time now if we want. We're canoe guys. She now has that expectation. There's no reason for her to suspect anything other than we're just guys who live on the lake out in our canoe."

I wonder how often I can canoe past her property without the dogs noticing me and without her wigging out.

CHAPTER 12

Becca

"What are they doing here?"

I nearly jump out of my shoes. I place my hand over my heart to make sure it remains in my chest. "You scared me to death! What are you sneaking up on me for?"

Grandma juts her gardening trowel in their direction. "They're the ones sneaking up on you."

I scoff. "Please, Gran. They're out on the lake. You should try it. Do you have a canoe or something I can go out on? It looks fun." I hope it's not totally obvious that I want to row over by their house to see what I can. And playing out on the lake this summer with cute Ben and his cute older brother seems like a perfectly fine idea.

She scoffs back. "None of this looked fun last week when you first moved here. Now all of a sudden 'let's play on the lake with the shirtless brothers.'" She mocks me and waggles her hips.

"Whatever." I turn to walk back to the barn, but she takes me by the upper arm.

"Becca, be careful."

"With what?"

She hasn't taken her eyes off the Hunt brothers' canoe. Come to think of it, neither has Morri. "Them."

She releases me and wanders back up to the house. I roll my eyes because old people are weird. But she's right. Suddenly the lake does seem a lot more appealing to me than it did before.

I observe the dogs some more and finish off my notes. Every now and then I wander down close to the dock, but stay back in the shade of the trees, as I try to find the lone canoe, but it's gone. Toward the end of the day, I see the blue canoe pulled up on a dock across the lake. Now I know which house is Ben's.

I was interested in him after he saved my life and saw him in all his cuteness in the dark. It seems to have increased significantly now that I've seen him basking in the summer sun, half dressed. Funny how that works.

I check on the dogs one last time before deciding I have enough information to pass today's training test, and locate Grandma in the living room settled in and watching what she calls her "programs," her feet propped up on the coffee table. She's drinking a tall glass of lemonade.

"Okay, I'm ready."

She points the remote at the TV like it's a magic wand and lowers the volume. "Shoot."

"Okay, there are five adults: Lugh, Meriden, Rhiannon, Angus, and Morrigan. There are eight puppies: Shannon, Bel, Cian, Dylan, Eostre, Gwyn, Teranis, and Olwen."

She corrects my pronunciation of Eostre. "Eostre, like Esther. And what else?"

"Lugh and Meriden must be mates, and Rhiannon and Angus are the puppies' parents."

"Correct."

"Morrigan is not an alpha. Lugh is and maybe... Rhiannon?"

"Correct."

"Other than Morri, I don't know who else may be a were-wolfhound."

"Correct."

"Correct? How is that correct?" Not that I should complain. This is the first test I've done well on since fifth grade.

"None of the others have shown to be were-wolfhounds, but I'm hoping some of the puppies, at least one, will," she explains.

"Okay." I'm feeling good about this journal thing today. I take a deep breath before continuing. "To get my attention, Morri will lean against me, put her head against my leg, lick at my hand, or paw me until I pet her or acknowledge her in some way."

"Good."

"I think that's it. Oh, and she isn't motivated by treats. She's motivated by approval and affection."

"Good."

"I don't know what else."

"How is she at catching?" Grandma grins at me.

"Terrible. You'd think a sight hound would be better at that."

"Well, the strength of a sight hound is to see things at a distance, like your boys in the boat—"

"Gran!"

"Her strength isn't to see tiny objects coming toward her. Tiny objects usually flee from her. She's a chaser, not a catcher."

"I can see that." I reach a hand out without looking and

pet her head. As she sits, her head is level with my hand without me having to bend down.

"Just now, you didn't look. You just pet her."

"Yeah, she's always right there, at my side."

"So you knew she'd be there."

I nod.

"How did you know she'd seen the boys on the lake?"

I tell Grandma how she growled and barked, how her ears went flat, how her body tensed, her hair spiked, and her tail stuck out.

She nods.

"How did she initially react to the ball, a seemingly new object to her?"

"Her ears went out to the side."

Gran smiles. "I call those their curious ears." She eyes me up and down and gives a quick side glance to Morrigan. "Okay, you did well today."

I clap my hands together. "Woot!"

"It's pass/fail, so I'd call that a pass. It wasn't a scholarly article, but it's a start."

"A D's a P!" I continue to dance around and celebrate.

"What does that mean?"

"A letter grade of D is still a pass. That's what I always say. No need to knock yourself out in school. The D average students are going to walk side-by-side with the A average students at graduation. No big diff."

"Honestly, Becca. I wouldn't go that far. Good grades can get you into better colleges," she argues.

"So can money and good looks. I'll take my chances! So, tomorrow, when do we start training Morrigan to fight!"

Gran laughs and shakes her head. "We don't train Morrigan, ever."

"What do you mean?"

She aims the magic remote control wand at the TV, turning it back up, signaling that she's pretty much done dealing with me. "The dogs know what to do. It's instinctive. We don't train the dogs. We train you."

CHAPTER 13

Becca

Mom comes home from work and tells us about all of the beautiful houses in the area and how her showings went at dinner. I half listen. I know I should be more interested in what she does, but I can't quit thinking about Ben. It's totally stupid, I know. I just saw the guy a few times. So there's a cute guy nearby. Big deal. I don't know. I don't know what it is. He's just on my mind. It's no big deal.

I listen as Grandma nods and responds to whatever Mom is saying. It's kinda nice sitting here with them and having dinner. But I miss Dad. He's texted me every day so far. I'll call him on the weekend, but it's not the same. With Mom and Dad together, though, we never all had dinner together. This is new. And I like it.

Maybe things weren't meant to be with Mom and Dad. That's life. Shit happens. They seemed happy. But what do I know about it? But really, how hard is it to have dinner together from time to time?

My mind fast-forwards to when I'm married with a kid

someday and how I'd sit down to dinner with my family. Of course, I can't imagine who'd cook the dinner because I can't cook, and it's sexist to expect that I'm the one slaving over the oven. My relationship would be different, and we'd have those gender stereotypes all worked out. Maybe there'd be a schedule or something on the fridge. But it wouldn't matter. He'd bring home takeout, then we'd go out to see an obscure indie band at a new bar after dinner, maybe drink too much, make out in the alley by the place, barely stand to wait all the way home to get in bed together. I imagine all of this going on, and picture my future generic husband pushing me up against the wall, unable to contain his desire for me, kissing me. He pulls away, and I see Ben's face.

"What the fuck?" I say out loud.

Mom and Grandma both turn and stare at me. Mom's eyebrows are raised. "Excuse me, Becca?"

I feel my face flush. "I'm sorry. I was thinking of something..."

"Watch your language," Mom chastises. Though it's interesting to note she never cared too much about my filthy mouth before moving in with her mother.

I know I shouldn't swear in front of Grandma though. It's disrespectful. "Sorry, I didn't mean it."

They go on (and on) about real estate. I try not to visualize my specific marriage future, but suffice it to say that my marriage would be fun and hot. All the time. Nonstop. And we'd have fucking dinner together.

I wonder if Ben likes David Bowie. Mom was lucky enough to see him in concert when she was around my age. She gave me the concert T-shirt from his show. Too late for me to see him now, but I love listening to his music.

SHAWNA ROMKEY

What is my deal? Who cares about Ben? My parents are getting a divorce, I've moved to this new podunk community, I'm switching schools. Again. And to top it all off, I have to kill monsters now. There's no time for boys. Boys are low priority. Not to mention, I'm going to be the weird, werewolf slayer, dog girl.

He's not into me. I happened to almost get killed while he was having dinner, and then he happened to be on the lake that he also lives on by my house.

Don't be an idiot, Becca. Put Ben out of your head. Never gonna happen. You've got too much other shit going on in your life. Let it go.

I wonder when I'll see him again.

I finish dinner and clean up, then head to my room. Morri follows along. My new shadow. I watch a show on Netflix on my computer and decide to rearrange my room so that I can see out my window from my bed.

Morri cocks her head as I rearrange, her curious ears to the side.

"To have a view of the lake!" I tell her. "That's all. The lake is nice!" I feel defensive, as though she's accusing me of wanting to look at Ben's house.

Mom opens the door while knocking softly on it. What was the point of that? Why knock and open? That prevented nothing. Come on in.

"What's all this about?" she asks.

"Just making this room feel like mine," I say.

She looks out the window. "This wouldn't happen to be about—"

"A view of the lake? Yes, that's what it is about. Geez."

She covers her mouth to hide her smile. "Okay. Mom told me about the Hunt boys."

I shrug. "What of it?"

"Nothing of it. I'm glad you're settling in and looking forward to getting out on the water." She helps me push the rest of the furniture in place. "How are you doing? You okay?"

I am okay, and almost feel guilty about being okay. "Yeah, I'm good." I flounce down on my bed and start untangling the earbuds for my phone.

She sits down on the end of the bed. "Mom said your training went well." She doesn't make eye contact when she says this, and the words come out sounding a bit sharp, if that makes sense. She must still have issues with it.

"Yeah, today it did."

"Good."

I should ask her about work or something, but she just spent thirty minutes talking about it, so I'm not sure what else to say. "How are you doing? Are you okay?"

She looks at the floor and nods. "Yeah," she says in a voice so quiet it sounds more like an intake of breath. Her eyes fill with tears. She means the opposite of "yeah."

I freeze, deer in headlights, gauge my surroundings, which way can I go? Headlights are coming right at me. Dart left? Dart right? Take them head-on.

She pats my leg, and looks away while taking a deep breath. "I'm okay. Good night, honey." She stands up.

The headlights veer around me.

"Good night, Mom." She leaves, and I put my headphones in.

I pat the bottom of the bed, and Morri jumps up, taking Mom's spot. I look out the window toward Ben's and let my 80s mix of Bowie, Prince, the Furs, and Yaz take control.

I gaze across the water to Ben's house. I survey the lake and the woods around it. A wolf attacked me the other day. A wolf from those woods. That's a big deal. Wolves shouldn't be this close to houses even though we are on the lake.

The lake backs up onto the Mark Twain National Forest. It's pretty big I guess, so the wolves *must* come from the woods. I stare into the dark thickness of the trees. If wolves are in the woods, what else might be in there?

CHAPTER 14

Becca

"And go!" Gran says, holding a whistle between her teeth and a stopwatch in her hand.

I do as many sit-ups as I can during the longest two minutes of my life until she tweets the whistle.

"Sixty," she says, though I know how many. I was counting. "Not bad. That's a pass. You only needed fifty-three."

"Great, are we done?" I know we're not. Grandma doesn't get all gussied up in shorts, a T-shirt, and a baseball hat for one two-minute test.

"Not yet." She smiles. "I'm giving you the US Army PT test. Sit-ups are the first one. Next are push-ups. After that, a run."

"Ugh."

"Assume the position," she says.

I give her a weirded-out look but get on all fours.

"Can you do boy push-ups?"

"Well, considering I'm a girl..."

"Try."

I go up on my hands and toes and don't wait for her to tell me to start. I do one boy push-up, grunting the whole way. After two more, I collapse onto my stomach.

"Switch to girl if you have to," she tells me. "Come on. It's just two minutes."

I do as many as I can, then she tweets the whistle again.

"Well, you did about thirty, but most of them weren't really up to standard. There was some sagging going on. I'm going to count fifteen."

"Whatever." I sit up and stretch my arms behind my back then up over my head.

"That's a fail, but it's okay. I didn't expect you to pass all of them the first day. These are a work in progress to get you in physical shape to keep up with Morrigan."

"Maybe I shouldn't have skipped gym class so much."

"Maybe not. Okay, get up and stretch a bit. You're going on a run around the lake."

"I'm not into running."

"You've got to be able to keep up or at least keep within sight of your were-wolfhound, Becca. Her life could depend on it. You're not only there to help her with the werewolves, if necessary. You're there to make sure she doesn't get killed."

"Yeah, well who's there to make sure I don't get killed?"

She smirks at me, but I really want to know.

"You're going to head down the street past Lake Pizza and the church. When you hit the community center parking lot, turn around and come back. I'm timing you."

"Great." I take a swig from my water bottle and stretch my quads. I give her a nod and take off.

74

Ben

I'm mowing Mr. Diller's lawn. The morning is a hot one already. I take my shirt off and wipe the sweat from my face with it. The lake will feel good later.

Then she runs by, her blonde hair in a ponytail that sticks out through the hole in the back of her baseball hat. God, she's beautiful. She runs like a gazelle, in a soft, easy stride. Her eyes stay on the road ahead of her, and she's breathing through her mouth. She's in a sports bra and a loose tank top. Her skin glistens in sweat. God, I need to get a grip.

She doesn't look over or seem to notice me, but I won't get that image of her out of my mind for as long as I live. This graceful creature running past me. Something inside me is triggered. I want to run after her. I want to give chase.

It's primal. It's biology. It's been bred into predators from the first spark of life. I don't want to hurt her though. I want to take her. I need her. I need to be close to her.

Jesus, I need to get a grip. She's passed by, but my blood is still rushing double time and my heart slamming to break out of my rib cage. I grip the handle of the mower hard and tense all of my muscles.

I don't even know anything about her. I feel so shallow. Oh, hot girl runs by. Big whoop. I've dated a few hot girls before. There are other hot girls who never flipped my switch like this. They were all fine and nice and whatever, but I was never driven to be with them. I never thought about them as I fell asleep or wondered about them when I first woke up in the morning. And this girl, Becca. I can't for the life of me get her out of my head, and now my body is urging me to go after her. It's ridiculous.

I continue mowing the lawn, and try to get my head back on task. This is bad. If she's a slayer, this is especially bad. I don't know what to do. Maybe I should tell Dad. Maybe he'd know what to do.

Becca

Oh, God. I wonder if he saw me. What am I doing running around the lake half dressed? I had no idea Grandma was going to make me parade around the community. Massive embarrassment.

But he took his shirt off that way guys do, reaching back over their head to pull it up and off. So hot when they do that. So then he was half dressed, too, and mowing the lawn. Sweaty, wiping the sweat with his shirt. I just got a glimpse of him before I realized it was him and averted my eyes, pretending not to see. Damn, he looks good without a shirt on. Damn, damn, damn.

My breathing pattern gets all out of whack, and I find it harder to catch my breath. My heart is already hammering like mad, mostly from the run but partly because of my nerves at seeing him. My pace quickens. I've got to run past him on the way back, too. How will I pretend not to see him?

God, he's hot. He makes me want to do unspeakable things to him.

Sweat is now pouring off me. I'm almost to the community center. I fast-forward a few songs on my iPhone and play something heavy. I've got to work off this pent-up energy. I run harder.

I make it to the community center in no time and turn around.

As I pass the place I'd seen Ben before, the mower sounds from around back. Thank God, thank God, thank God. He doesn't have to see me, and I don't have to see him and get all worked up over him.

The image of him, all shirtless and sweaty, isn't helping me stop thinking about him.

Maybe I should just ask him out. Maybe we should just do something and see what happens.

I've only gone out with a couple guys before, and things never amounted to much. There was never a spark or a real desire to go on a second date. They'd ask, and I'd be busy until I'd move again.

But Ben... I could just eat him up. God!

I crank up my jams and run back to Grandma's, much faster and harder than I'd started my run.

CHAPTER 15

Becca

"Not bad. Eighteen minutes, twenty-two seconds," Grandma says as I lean over, hands on my knees as I catch my breath. "Walk it off a little."

I do so, panting like crazy, and take a drink from my water bottle. "That...sucked," I say between breaths.

"You'll get used to it."

I take my iPhone off the strap on my upper arm, set it on the picnic table, then walk toward the dock.

"Where are you going?"

It takes too much of my air to reply, so I just keep going until I'm at the end, then I dive in. Cold, cold, cold! The lake hasn't warmed up for the summer yet, but it's a good cold. It's a cold I need after that run, after seeing Ben in jeans without a shirt and the sweat...

I come up for air and feel better. Morri has run down to the end of the dock and whimpers, looking after me.

"I'm okay, Morri."

Her tail wags.

I climb up the ladder and get out immediately. I needed the refreshing dip, but I didn't need to linger.

"That's all we have today," Grandma tells me.

"Okay."

"We'll be doing those every week until you stay at the level I think you should be. Before you go, though, come with me real quick," she says.

I nod to conserve my air, which is slowly coming back to my lungs.

She opens up the barn and flips on the lights. "Head up the ladder," she instructs.

"Ugh, really, Gran?" I don't have the energy for this, but I do it.

"Open up the cabinet along the back wall and pick one," she says.

I get to the top and wade through the hay stored there for the dog beds. It sticks to my wet ankles as I pass. I like the smell of it in here. It's a good farm smell of hay and clean air. It wasn't bad in the city with pollution, but it wasn't like this. I open up the cabinet and see a massive collection of weaponry.

"Gran!"

She hasn't climbed up with me, but looks up at the loft. "Choose your weapon."

"I thought you said I didn't need to fight, that I was the sidekick and Morrigan did all the heavy lifting."

"I did, but in case Morrigan isn't there or is incapacitated or you are surrounded, you need to have something other than her."

I run my hands along the various weapons stored in the rustic cabinet. Most of them are held up on the pegboard backing. Guns, knives, daggers, swords, clubs, bows and arrows, and crossbows.

"This is nuts," I say. I had no idea my grandmother had a weapons stash.

"Take a close-range and long-range weapon. You should train with one of each. Don't think too hard about it. Just take whatever you're drawn to."

I select a long dagger that stands out to me. It's sharp, obviously, but it has a floral hilt, which strikes me as clashing with its purpose. Then I look at a crossbow. I take it off the board and look down at Grandma.

She smiles. "Good picks. You'll start with them tomorrow."

At dinner, Mom tells us of her real estate excitement for the day again, and I try to be interested. But I'm training to be a werewolf slayer, after all, and that's way more exciting.

At a break in the conversation, I say, "So what were your weapons, Gran?"

Mom dabs her mouth with her napkin and clears her plate from the table.

Grandma looks at her while answering me. "Oh, I liked the dagger and the pistol, myself."

Mom excuses herself and goes into the living room.

"Pistol? Really?"

"Yes, but the sound can draw attention to you. Each weapon has advantages and disadvantages. The crossbow is quiet, but can take time to load. You can get quick with it, but seconds can make all the difference."

I nod and take a bite of my pork roast. "So how long will I be training?"

"Well, you'll train until you retire. It's a lifelong commitment. I want to take you through at least eight weeks of slayer boot camp before I take you out to see any real danger."

"Real danger? Like, what, you're going to take me to a werewolf lair?" I'm excited and scared shitless all at the same time.

She squints and tilts her head from side to side. "Not exactly, but we'll go on some hunts. I want you ready before you start school."

I don't ask why. It makes sense. My training time will be seriously hindered by high school.

"Eight weeks doesn't seem to be enough," she says, not really directed at me but to the ether. "There's so much you need to know."

"Like what?"

She takes a deep breath. She's finished her meal, while I get seconds. The running has made me seriously hungry.

"Let's start with the werewolf lore. Werewolves are cursed by demons. Demons curse humans with lycanthropy and use them as minions for larger demons or even the Devil himself, it is said. Lycanthropy can be cured two ways: by a spell that breaks the curse or an exorcism. The Roman Catholic Church was big on handling them back in Ireland during their first infestation but aren't as involved with werewolves today."

"So the goal is to cure them?"

She laughs. "Well, the goal for some people is, but we are slayers, not curers."

"So how do we slay them?"

"Pretty much like you'd slay anything."

"Do I need silver-tipped arrows or garlic or anything?"

She laughs. "No, those are myths. Some hunters use silver for a kick or a nod to the myth, but silver isn't necessary. What we focus on, the deadliest thing to a werewolf, is the bite of a wolfhound. When the saliva from the wolfhound gets in a werewolf's bloodstream, it's fatal within minutes."

"Nice." I look down to my right where Morrigan is ever-present. "Cool drool, girl."

She, of course, wags her tail.

"A wolfhound's bite can cure an innocent, but if the person beneath the curse has been corrupted, they'll be immune to a cure. The wolfhound must take them down." Gran appears to be deep in thought as she explains all of this.

"What makes one werewolf an innocent and another corrupted?"

"An innocent hasn't killed anyone yet. The corrupted one has."

"Soooo, does that mean some werewolves are good and try not to kill anyone, or does that mean they just haven't had the opportunity yet?" I take the last bite of my dinner and push my plate to the side.

She sighs. "Good question. That is a point of contention within the clans and within the Church. What makes them evil and corrupt? Are they evil from the moment of the curse? Can they fight the effects? Should we try to cure them first?" She shrugs. "I don't know. My *modus operandi* has always been to kill on sight. Shoot first, ask questions later."

"Well, what if they are fighting the curse? What if they are innocent people like you or me who've gotten cursed, but want to be cured?"

Grandma looks at me, her eyes narrowed. "Werewolves killed your grandfather, Becca, in front of me. Now I kill werewolves."

I lean back in my chair, my eyes wide. I've been questioning their existence all this time, and here she is having been up close and personal, having lost someone she loved right in front of her. Why hadn't I been told? Why did no one ever mention any of this to me?

"I...I'm sorry." I back away from the conversation and the table to put my plate in the dishwasher.

"Some other things you should know, the older the werewolves are, the more they can control their shifting. Young werewolves are prone to acting in a rabid, feral manner.

"There is a hierarchy in a pack, with an alpha, beta, omega, and a loner.

"Wolfhounds are sight hounds and can spot werewolves from great distances. They can also smell and hear them, but sight is their greatest asset. Their size and fighting style are perfect for taking a werewolf down.

"Wolfhounds act like a typical dog, as you've seen, unless a werewolf is within range. If they see a werewolf in full form, you'll know it. They go wild and turn from domesticated dog to dangerous beast, like you saw with the wolf Morrigan killed in front of you. Werewolves in hybrid form, while in the midst of shifting, get the same treatment. Werewolves in human form are a bit trickier. The wolfhound can sense something is off, but they aren't motivated to kill unless directed to, or unless the human acts aggressively. In these cases, the handler has to take over against humans, or give direct commands to the hound on what to do. All of which is another reason for you to train with the weapons."

I lean against the counter. "So, where is the magic spell to cure them?"

"The spells come from witches, usually witches of the Celtic line."

My mind is reeling. I only found out about werewolves

being real last week, and now demons and witches are added to the supernatural soup.

"Do you have the spell?"

"I don't have it, and if I did, it wouldn't matter. Casting it would require practice and training from a witch."

"Do you know a witch?" My voice rises in pitch.

"I can find a witch if I need one."

I run my hands through my hair. This is all so crazy. "I mean, if there's a cure for lycan…whatever you call it, why don't we work on a massive spell to cure werewolves? It seems like it'd be so much easier."

"Becca, I'm going to stop you right there. I'm training you to kill them, not cure them. If you want to cure them, I'm not the trainer for you."

At that, she gets up from the table and walks away. I guess my lesson is over for today.

Ben

"It's fend for yourself night," Sam says as he sits on the couch, feet propped up on the table as he chows down on a giant sub from Lake Pizza.

"What else is new?" I grumble and search the fridge for something to eat. I've showered and am ready to relax for the night. I've been mowing lawns all afternoon, so I'm starving. Nothing in the fridge, as usual.

"Dad should be home soon," Nic says as he walks by me and grabs his keys. "I'm out for the night. Don't do anything stupid, dumbasses." He tosses the keys in the air, catches them, and he's out the door.

I resent being lumped into the dumbass category with my brother. Sam is most definitely a dumbass. I, however, make good grades, help people in the neighborhood, coach little league soccer....

"Hey, dillhole, grab me a Coke, would ya?"

I close my eyes and shake my head. Why was I cursed with Sam as a brother? Nic I could live with. If it were only him and me, we'd be good. Sam is just a total pain in my ass when he's around. I grab him a Coke anyway and toss it to him in the living room.

He catches it, barely even looking in the direction it came from. He doesn't thank me, of course.

I scour the fridge again, hoping something may have magically appeared that I missed, but if both my brothers have been here all afternoon, the likelihood of there being any food anywhere within a five-mile radius is slim to zilch.

I hear Dad drive up and pray he brought food of some kind. I remain pathetically looking in the fridge as he enters in the hopes that he'll pity me if he hasn't already brought food and go buy something. He doesn't disappoint. He enters, balancing two pizza boxes in his right hand and carrying his toolbox in the other.

"Hey, boys! I brought some za!"

"Thank God," I say and snatch the top box from his hands.

"You don't have to go so far as to call me God. Dad will suffice."

"Wow, a dad joke," I say, not laughing.

In seconds both boxes are on the table, and I've nabbed three pieces and taken them away to put on my own plate like a wild animal taking his share from the carcass and carrying it off from the others to eat it. I've dibbed them, and Sam can't take them now that I'm safely away from the box, but he remains with his sub. It's a pretty big sub.

"Did you work today?" Dad asks.

I tell him about the Dillers' and the Hubbards' lawns between bites, mostly.

He sits down and has some pizza with me, but eats it at a much slower rate than I do.

"You're home early," I say.

He nods. "I am. Wanted to talk to you a bit."

Dammit, Nic.

"Oh? About what?"

He takes a deep breath, and I keep eye contact with the quickly disappearing pizza in the box. "Nic says there's a girl."

What an understatement. There's a girl, all right. There's a girl that only extreme hunger had got me to stop thinking about for a few minutes. There's a girl who's taken residence in my head. There's a girl who triggers a physical need inside me that I've never felt before. There's a girl who might also be a supernatural werewolf killer, and if I had any sense at all, I would stay far away from her.

"A girl?" Always best to play dumb. Parents and girls always easily believe it. Often because it's true.

"The new girl at Mrs. Russell's?"

I take a huge bite to stall replying. "Oh, yeah." I chew.

"Well?"

"Well what? I don't have anything to do with what happens at Mrs. Russell's."

He puts his pizza down. "Ben, look at me."

I hate when he does this. I finish chewing and look at him.

"You know how serious this is."

I shrug.

"Ben, we have a truce with the Russells."

"Dad." I swallow and wipe my mouth with the back of my hand. "I'm not violating any truce. If anything, I helped it. I pushed her out of the way of the LaRettes' truck. I saved her life!"

"I know. Nic told me."

"That douche."

"Ben," he chastises me. "You know the terms."

"Dad, I stayed away from their property. This all happened by Lake Pizza."

"And on the lake behind their house?"

I inhale deeply and drop my pizza on my plate in a huff. "We were just trying to see—"

"Ben!" He raises his voice. "Don't piss down my back and tell me it's raining! Stay away from her."

"She may not be a slayer," I say, my voice low.

"It doesn't matter! Ben! We agreed to stay away from Helen Russell and her business, and she stays away from us and ours. If that pact is broken, do you know what could happen?"

I shrug like I don't care. But I know. And I do actually care.

"She and those dogs could hunt down both you and your brother."

"They could hunt half of me," I say under my breath.

"Do you think that woman cares? I know you look over there and you see some old lady, but she's been hunting longer than I've been alive! Werewolves got her husband. She is no friend to lycanthropes, I can assure you. Her dogs are bred from ancient lines of werewolf killers. Their instinct and hers is to kill on sight.

"It took a great deal of communicating with her when we moved in and her dogs first picked up your scent. The only reason you and Sam are still alive is that you were only a child and you were human when her dogs came upon you."

"I'm always human," I say, which is mostly true.

"You were children, so she had mercy. You're men now. If she sees you sniffing around her granddaughter, you are done."

"I'm not sniffing—"

"Ben, you are done! Do you hear me?"

I avert my gaze again and nod.

"Do we have to move?" he asks.

"What? No!"

"I'm serious, Ben. Do we have to move?"

He eyes me, his brows raised, and Sam stands in the doorway watching. He doesn't have a dumbass look or a smirk on his face for once. He's waiting for my answer, and his eyes are serious, which never happens. The weight of that hits me. This is all extremely real.

"No."

"This is life and death. Not just for you."

"Dad, the LaRettes went after her—"

"That's fine. You can mess with the LaRettes if you want. Just stay away from anything Connolly Clan related, and that includes that girl."

"Becca," I say and realize it was a mistake.

He takes my chin and forces me to meet his eyes. "Forget her name. Forget *her*. Do you understand me?"

I nod. I do understand. I just don't agree.

He pushes away from the table and heads to his room.

He doesn't understand that there's no way I can forget her.

CHAPTER 16

Becca

I suck with these weapons. I'd switch to using Grandma's guns, but I'd have to go to the shooting range to practice those, so the crossbow is more accessible. I'm just going to need more practice.

Grandma tries her best to train me. She's set up a bale of hay down by the dock for me to practice with, and she's given me the gist of how to aim and fire. I'll probably need to look up some YouTube videos on this to supplement though.

Morri lies patiently in the shade watching. She's always there watching with her curious ears out to the side. We spend an hour or so playing tug-of-war and catch, which she sucks at beyond belief. Good thing werewolves haven't figured out they could just throw stuff at her and whatever it was would bounce off her head.

While I practice shooting, Grandma sometimes works with Morri, throwing things for her to fetch and play-fighting with her big, padded arm, like the police use to train dogs. Grandma says the dogs don't need much training. It's instinct. She thinks Morri is good to go. She thinks I, however, need work.

But I've done the PT tests and am improving. Morri and I are clearly bonded. It's just that things are getting a bit boring. I don't see the point. I mean, Gran says there are werewolves out there, but part of me still doesn't truly believe it. I may never see one, so what's the point of all this work?

Twang. My bolt misses the bale entirely.

"Okay, let's take a lunch break," Grandma says, carrying over some food. A pitcher of lemonade is already set.

"Gladly," I mutter and take the crossbow to the picnic table.

"Ah ah ah! No weapons on my table!"

I lean it next to me. "I'll figure it out."

"I know you will." She smiles and sits across from me.

I eat and don't mention how bored I am. I think about getting a part-time job. Maybe I'll check out the pizza place.

Okay, now I'm lying to myself. I make sure to run by Lake Pizza every day and then take Morri there on our walks, too. I don't even like pizza that much, but that's where I first saw Ben, so maybe he goes there often?

"Maybe for dinner, I'll go get us some pizza," I say in my most helpful tone.

Grandma sees through it because helpful isn't my go-to. "You're hoping to see him there again, aren't you?"

"See who?"

"Ben Hunt. Becca, darling, I told you, he's not a good idea."

I don't know what she even means. He's not an idea.

He's a guy. A cute guy who saved me and sometimes canoes and mows lawns without a shirt.

"Huh?"

"Becca, I didn't want to tell you this, but I guess I need to. The Hunts aren't good people."

I frown. "What?"

"I asked you to stay away from them the other day when we saw them on the lake. Now I'm telling you. You have to stay away from that boy. They have ties…to certain things."

"What, like mob ties?"

"No, like lycanthrope ties." She meets my gaze like she's daring me to argue.

"Lycanthrope ties. What does that mean?"

She sighs and shakes her head, looking down at her plate. "I don't know. It means the dogs get twitchy by their place. Brigid was wild one night we walked by there years ago. I think she'd have torn someone apart if I'd let her. There's a werewolf in that house."

"That's insane!"

"Becca, it's not insane."

"Gran, if you don't want me dating, then say so. You don't have to make up crazy stories to scare me away. If I didn't know any better, I'd think Dad put you up to it."

"No one put me up to it, Becca. I know these things, and one day you will, too. You'll know the dogs, and you'll know Morrigan and what she senses. Eventually you'll know her so well that you'll sense it too. Ten years ago at least, there was a werewolf in that house. I know it."

"Then why didn't you do anything about it?"

Grandma takes a bite and pauses for what seems like for. Ever. "Because I'm pretty damn sure it was those boys."

"Nope, nuh-uh. This is ridiculous."

"Becca, their father begged me to let it go. He promised me they would keep to themselves and stay away from us if we did the same. He promised he'd be an ally."

"Great! Problem solved. They're our allies."

"No, Becca. I don't trust them. The curse of lycanthropy is demonic. You can't just play nice. You can't just be an ally. You kill whether you want to or not. The moon controls you. The curse twists you."

"Gran, you said that some are innocent."

"I don't believe it. Some do."

"Well, maybe you should just try. I didn't believe any of it, and you made me."

"Becca." Her voice starts to crack. "I've seen what lycanthropy does to good people. Good people." She takes both of my hands and looks at me. "I saw what it did to your grandfather." A tear falls down her cheek. Before I can ask about it or get the details, she says, "You have to stay away from that boy. It's life and death. I forbid you from seeing him again."

My grandpa wasn't just killed by werewolves? He *was* a werewolf?

I reach out to her and put my hand on hers. It's hard when adults cry. I'd kind of thought that once I was done being a teenager, I'd stop crying when I was upset, but Mom does it a lot lately, and now Grandma. My stomach tightens.

She's crying, so I just nod. While learning that there's more to the story of my grandfather's death is significant, I'm surprised at how little my grandmother knows me. She just forbade me from seeing him? That was the exact wrong path to take to get me to fall in line. He just became 1000 percent more appealing.

It's getting dark. I sneak out for a walk without Morrigan. I get past Grandma without her noticing me, but my dog is much more perceptive. She is tall enough to watch me out the front windows and see me leave the yard. Luckily she stands there, ears to the sides, and doesn't bark or whine. I make my escape.

I walk the road to Lake Pizza, but I've been here so many times that Ben hasn't, so my expectations are low. Either way, I could get a Diet Coke and some fresh air. Mom and Grandma don't get along the best, so it's good to get out of the house. They don't argue so much as just have this air of tension that hangs between them constantly. Mom and Dad kinda had that, too. And now that I think about it, so do Mom and I. I wonder if it's just that Mom can't get along with anyone.

I feel bad thinking that. The separation wasn't her fault. Or maybe it was. What do I know? They haven't told me anything. They just rearrange me and set me up and relocate me wherever they need to so their lives can be more comfortable. Never mind mine.

I head into Lake Pizza. It's brightly lit, all red and white, and is an attempt to recreate some sort of retro 50s feel. A few people are behind the counter and a few tables have customers, but none of them are Ben. Whatever. I don't really see the point in a relationship anyway. Gran is probably right. I don't think the Hunts are werewolves, but there's probably something about him. He probably drinks too much, or has a crazy ex, or makes fun of unpopular people at school. What do I really know about him?

And let's say he doesn't have any of those flaws. What's the point? Like we'll be together forever? Stupid. Like my parents thought? Like half the married people in the world thought? And the other half are probably just unhappy but stubborn. Who knows? Marriage is stupid. Marriage is a sexist overthrow from a time when women couldn't work and needed protection and our life spans were only forty years. Forever meant like fifteen years, so whatever. But now, you get married and you're stuck forever. Stuck with some imperfect person who is stuck with an imperfect you. Like my parents. Then you have kids who are stuck with your imperfect relationship and have to pay the price.

I walk up to the counter. A cheery girl with multi-colored hair pulled back in a ponytail behind her visor looks at me. She has nerdy glasses and a shit ton of bangles and rubber bracelets on her right wrist.

"Hi! What can I get ya?" she asks with so much perkiness I think I can taste sugar.

"Oh, hi, uhhhh…."

An older guy brushes past me and leans on the counter in front of her. He looks like he's in his early twenties and is dressed in typical Missouri trucker fashion. Trucker hat, T-shirt, plaid work shirt over the T-shirt even though it's a thousand degrees out, work boots, dirty finger nails. "Maddie, honey. Come on. What are you doing after work?"

Her fake smile cracks, but she maintains eye contact with me and doesn't acknowledge him. Her brows rise as though to encourage me to speak.

"I think I'll just have a Diet Coke."

"Maddie!" he barks at her. "Come on, darling. When are you off work?"

She takes a deep breath and slowly turns from me. "Are you seriously hitting on a girl wearing a visor? I'm at work, Teddy. And even if I weren't, ewwww. You're engaged. Get out and go home to your fiancée." She composes herself with a deep breath and turns back to me. "I'm sorry, what—"

He slams his fist down on the counter, and she jumps. I don't.

"Dude!" I say, slowly turning to glare at him. "I'm ordering here. Why don't you take a walk?"

He turns his attention to me, and his eyes narrow. "Who the fuck do you think you are, little girl?" His nostrils flare, and he looks so hard at me I think he sees through me.

I don't know if it's my training or what, but his attitude makes me want to kick the shit out of him. I know all I've done is some running and calisthenics, and I don't have a weapon on me or a big ass dog at my hip, but my blood burns, and I want to take this loser out, right here, right fucking now.

I take a ready stance and square off with him, my right foot slightly back. I pull my right hand back to prepare a punch. "I think I'm Becca fucking Redford, and I'm gonna make you cry in front of this nice girl here."

So yeah, I've never been in a fight before. I may have gotten angry and kicked a chair or screamed while driving to blow off steam, but I have no clue how to fight or why I soooo want to take this guy out, but I feel pretty confident I can do it.

He leans back, and his eyes widen. He assesses my posture. I can see the whites of Maddie's eyes in my peripheral vision. Then he laughs, and I can't even fucking deal with that. He laughs so hard he holds his belly like his guts are going to spill out if he doesn't hold them in, and I'm itching to make that happen. I pull back and punch him across the face. Like I've seen in movies and on TV. I hit him as hard as I can, and his face seems to smush in slow motion.

But fuck! Ow! Fuck fuck fuck, punching hurts. "Ow, shit!" I say, and turn to shake out my hand.

His jaw must be made of concrete. I start jumping around and try not to cry, but I think I broke something. Maybe even several somethings.

He slowly turns back to me and straightens up from the counter he'd had his elbows on. He's big. He's like 6'5", broad chest, big arms. Good choice to pick for my first fight. Way to go, Becca.

Maddie stands there, straight as a fence post, jaw hanging open.

I have a feeling my face is about to hurt worse than my hand.

"Well, Little Miss Redford, I'm going to have to answer that." He pulls back.

I should run, but instead I brace for impact and close my eyes.

"Whoa! Whoa! Whoa!" someone says, and I hear scrambling and movement in front of me. "Hold on there, Teddy."

I open one eye to see Ben standing between us and a few guys pulling Teddy away from me.

"What the hell ya doin'? Gonna hit a girl in the middle of Lake Pizza?" Ben asks.

I don't like that he referred to me as a girl, though I am. It just seems as if he meant I was inferior or something. I do, however, like the fact that he just kept that guy from breaking my face. My hand throbs.

Teddy shakes his head quickly, as though to wake himself up. "No."

"Good," one of the other guys says. "Because that would be a very big mistake." He pats Teddy's back with one hand but is holding him by the shoulder with the other. "Why don't you run home to Judith, and have a beer."

Teddy nods, but then narrows his eyes at me. "I'll see you later."

"Can't wait," I sass back. But I can. I can wait a really long time for that.

The other guy escorts Teddy out the front door, and Maddie scrambles and hands me a Diet Coke. "Here, on the house."

I reach for it with my smashed hand, but it just hangs limply. "Thanks."

Ben holds my upper arms so he can look me in the eyes. "Are you okay?"

"I think I'm gonna…" And everything goes black.

Ben

"Oh my God!" Sam bends over laughing. "That was fucking hilarious! Did you see her?"

I'm holding her in my arms. She fainted right into me. I ease her down to the ground, her head in my lap. God, she smells like vanilla and lilacs. I have a nose for scents. Her blonde hair spills around her face onto my leg, and I don't think I've ever been happier. Or more scared. Or more impressed. Or more confused in my life.

"She just fucking clocked him right in the jaw. Fucking Teddy LaRette! Do you believe that chick?"

Nic comes in, and the door closes behind him. "We should get her to the clinic."

He's right. I know he's right. But I don't want to move. Ever. From this spot with her lying on me. "Yeah." I don't really know what to do next.

"I'll help you get her up," Nic says. Always so take charge and by the book. He and Sam couldn't be any more different. How the three of us are brothers is beyond me.

Maddie runs over with a cold cloth and blots Becca's head. "I'll go grab some ice for that hand." She takes off to the back of the kitchen.

We maneuver Becca into a booth. I've taken over the forehead blotting duties, but still make sure to get into the booth first, so she's still leaning on me.

"She probably passed out from the pain," Nic says.

"Oh my God, did you see that?" Sam asks again. His laughs are fading.

"Yeah," Nic says, as he eyes her seriously.

"What?" I ask. He's thinking something.

He looks around. The other customers are back to their pizzas and not paying attention, but he still frowns and strokes his chin. "That was Teddy LaRette."

I nod. "Yeah, I know. So?"

He shakes his head, his gaze remaining on her.

Maddie hurries to our side and gives us a bag of frozen French fries for Becca's hand. "It's the best we got."

"Thanks, Madeline." Nic smiles at her.

She stares at him, and her breath catches in a little gasp. He has that effect on girls. Lucky bastard.

"No problem whatsoever." She stands there smiling for a few more seconds then seems to remember she was working, and heads back to the counter.

"Nic, what is it?" I press.

"You saw how quick she was to hit him?"

"Oh my God!" That sets Sam off into fits again.

"Yeah, so?" Then I clue in to what he's getting at. "Oh, come on, Nic."

"You saw her!"

I lower my voice in case she comes out of it. "Nic, Teddy LaRette is a dick of the highest caliber. I hardly think someone being provoked to want to punch him in the face is a rarity."

He responds with his voice even lower. "The LaRettes are werewolves, Ben. He gave her one reason, and she snapped. I saw her from the doorway. That was rage, and it welled up from her feet to her fist. That was wild, primal, and instinctive."

"Nic." I want to stop him. I want him to just stop talking. I don't want her to be a slayer. I want her to be the hot girl on the other side of the lake, not the girl who is driven to murder me. "Don't give me this werewolf slayer bullshit again."

"Oh no, Ben. I think it's worse than that."

"What are you talking about?" But please stop talking.

"She's not only a werewolf slayer. She's a sister of the moon."

Becca

I wake up in Ben's arms. He's warm, and I don't want to move. Another guy looks on, eyes wide. I hope I didn't do anything stupid. My hand throbs, and I realize I did.

"Shit." I sit up and turn to Ben in the booth. "I'm so sorry."

"No, it's okay. Really," he says.

I miss his warmth already. "My hand really hurts."

This snaps wide-eyed guy into action. Another guy stands there and covers his mouth to hold in a laugh.

"Oh, uh, Becca. This is Nic and Sam. My brothers," Ben says.

"Well, I'd shake your hand, but mine is broken at the moment," I say, hoping to sound funny and not bitchy.

"Right, let's get you to the med center. We can drive you," Ben says.

"Oh." He's probably right. I should have it looked at. But Grandma just forbade me from seeing him and all. "Yeah, good idea."

Ben holds the door for me as I cradle my injured hand, balancing a bag of frozen fries on it for some reason. Sam goes to the passenger side of the truck.

"I got this, Sam," Ben says and gives Sam a pointed look.

Sam steps back and holds both hands up in surrender, then turns and heads down the road.

"You got it? You sure?" Nic eyes me strangely.

"Yeah," Ben says with a tinge of exasperation. "It's a mile away. I can handle it."

I get butterflies in my stomach. He's trying to be alone with me. He's trying to ditch his brothers and take care of me. My heart starts pounding so hard my injured hand starts to throb.

He comes over and opens the passenger door for me, which is good because I can't do it.

I get nervous butterflies again. I'm in his truck, his green Ford Ranger. I'm in Ben's truck. He's driving me somewhere. I've been invited into his world. I see that it's pretty clean, for a guy's truck. When he turns the key, the classic rock station plays some Aerosmith. He puts his seat belt on, and I turn for mine, then realize I can't grab it with my hand.

"Oh."

He looks over. "Excuse my reach," he says and leans across me for the belt.

He's warm again and smells good. Earthy and like a guy. I notice him inhale deeply when he's near me. He seems to take a second or two too long as he reaches across me, but that's okay. I kind of smile and resist the urge to pull him into me because that would be inappropriate, and it would hurt my hand. He stretches the belt across me and clicks it into the buckle.

"There," he says and looks at me.

Our eyes meet and neither of us looks away for a second. I want to kiss him so bad.

He looks away. "So yeah, the med center." He starts the truck and drives me down the street.

He waits with me until they can see me, then stays in the waiting room while they work on me. The doctor splints my hand. Three hairline fractures.

I come out to see Grandma and Mom just arriving through the sliding emergency doors. The first thing Mom looks at is my splint. The first thing Grandma looks at is Ben Hunt.

"What did you do?" she accuses him.

"Gran, he drove me here to get my hand looked at," I say.

"And he called us to get her," Mom adds. "God forbid she actually call us herself."

"How did this happen?" Grandma asks Ben.

"Uhhh...."

"I did this," I interject. "I hit some douche face at Lake Pizza."

Ben spits out a laugh and quickly covers his mouth. Grandma glares.

"Sorry," Ben says, "but she's right. Teddy LaRette is a douche face."

A man enters but remains in the doorway of the med clinic. He's dressed in jeans and a flannel shirt. He's tall and lean and has stubble across his chin. "Ben, let's go. Now."

He's a good-looking man. I notice Mom stare at him a little too long.

"Mrs. Russell, I'm very sorry," he says to Grandma. "Won't happen again."

"Dad—" Ben protests.

"Sorry for what?" I blurt out.

The man purses his lips and smiles politely, then gives Grandma another serious look before grabbing Ben by his shirt and pushing him out the door. Ben gives me an understated wave before he's out of sight.

"Bye," I say feebly, then turn to Grandma. "What the hell? He didn't do anything but help me after I hurt myself, and he kept me from getting my face smashed in. He brought me here. Why do you have to treat him like that?"

"Becca, get in the damn car right now."

We drive home in silence. First thing I do when I get inside, other than pet Morri with my left hand, is take a pain pill the doctor gave me.

Grandma refuses to look at me. She paces the kitchen furiously, her mouth clamped shut. I've never seen her like this. She's the one who always spoiled me and gave me extra banana cream pie after dinner when I was a kid. She always bought a bunch of toys for me at the dollar store. She let me have ice cream for breakfast. She did all the things Mom wanted her not to. Not today.

"Jessica, do something or I will!" she says to Mom.

"For what? Punching that guy? Sounds like he deserved it," Mom says. Pretty much the only time she defends me is if it's against Dad or Grandma.

"For disobeying me! I told her not to see those Hunt boys. And by the way, who says the LaRette kid deserved it? We don't go walking around punching jerks in the face." She turns on me. "Did he do something to you? Did he touch you? Did he hurt someone?"

I jut my chin out. "Well, not really. He was kinda harassing the girl at the counter."

"So you punched him?" Mom asks, and I can see her loyalties are turning.

I shrug.

"Did he say something rude or hurt her?" Mom seems to be giving me an opportunity to justify my actions.

"I don't think so. He slammed his hand on the counter."

Grandma has stilled and stares at me. She tilts her head to the side. "Wait, you punched him for slamming his hand on the counter?"

"Go on, Morri!" I say to the dog. She is sniffing me like crazy. My jeans, my shirt. "What is your deal?" I shove her away with my knee.

Grandma zeroes in on Morrigan now, too. Her eyes start darting around wildly, looking up and around like she's searching for something. She turns and heads to the den without saying anything.

"What's with her?" I ask Mom.

She takes a deep breath. "Who knows? You should try to respect her wishes though. We are in her house."

"Mom, her wishes are out of line. She wants me to stay away from the only person my age I've met here. I mean, we've moved again. My dad is somewhere else. I have no friends but this big derpy idiot here." I gesture to Morri with my good hand. She's now frantically sniffing my injured hand but seems to take care not to touch it. "I mean, I finally find someone I could hang out with, and she wants to forbid it. Like, who does that? Are we in the Middle Ages or something?"

"I know, honey. I'm sorry for all you've been put through."

"I'm going to bed. My hand hurts like hell."

I head up to my room to lie down. The medicine is making me tired already.

The landline rings downstairs, and before I can fall asleep in my bed, Grandma busts in through my door. "Bring Morrigan. We need to go. There's been a murder."

CHAPTER 17

Ben

Ever since Mom was turned, Dad has been on the hunt. You wouldn't think he's a particularly educated guy, but when he wants to find something out, he'll research and read up on it for hours. It's appropriate that werewolves and our lore are high on his list.

So when he tells me to get in his truck to go check out a sighting, I go without question.

Mom's conversion when she was pregnant with me was hard on him. At the time, he didn't understand it, didn't know about werewolves at all, and was helpless. When she tried to leave after I was born and take all of us boys to her pack, he tried to stop her with a double-barreled shotgun. She pulled a typical movie super villain trick, making Dad choose which of his children wouldn't get turned, Sam or Nic. She held me, just a baby, and threatened to claw me. She clawed Sam because he was within reach, infecting him with the disease, while Dad did what he could to save Nic, who was closest to him.

It all happened so fast.

Little did we know, I was already infected, having been in the womb when she turned.

But since then, he's been reading and looking for information on how to cure us, as well as how to contain us during the moon. The full moon. The only moon that counts as far as he's concerned. But I can tell you, the other phases hit us in different ways. Dark moons tend to make me more secretive, reclusive. I want to hide and avoid others during dark moons. Then as the moon starts to wax, I feel the wolf inside me start to yawn and stretch, start to want to come out and howl and run and attack. I try to push it down all the time, suppress it, fight it. Full moons are the hardest, but I feel the wolf during every phase.

Neither Sam nor I has bitten or clawed and definitely hasn't killed anything but other werewolves in our werewolf forms. Technically, according to lore, you need to commit a violent act against a pure human in wolf form for lycanthropy to take full hold. Some like Mrs. Russell probably see us as dangerous and evil as full werewolves who go on killing sprees. We have abilities. We are dangerous. We just aren't murderers...yet.

But Dad has worked with us on meditation, self-control, and the odd chaining us in the basement when necessary. The basement thing happens to Sam more than me.

And he has made it his mission to stop any werewolves he comes across. I sometimes suspect he's searching them out in hopes of finding Mom again, but I can't say for sure. We know of the LaRettes, but have a pact with them, too. They keep to themselves. They don't turn people. There are no reports of them hurting anyone, so Dad leaves them alone. We suspect they travel to do their damage, but right now it's not in our backyard, so we leave them be.

But when the radio scanner goes off and there's a mauling, he takes bizarre interest in having a look. Maybe it's Mom. Maybe it's the LaRettes. Maybe it's a new pack in town. He'll find out.

Butting up against the lake is a huge area set aside as part of the Mark Twain National Forest. One of the reasons we moved here is that the forest is a hub for lycanthropic activity, and of course, it's rumored Mom's pack lives somewhere in the heart of the woods. A small corner of it lies right between the lake and my school. I've been told not to walk through those woods since I was a little kid. There have been lots of "animal sightings," the authorities say. But we know the truth.

Dad's headlights bounce around the road that's badly in need of repair. They illuminate different areas each time they leap. I keep waiting for a video game jump scare to pop up in one of them.

"This isn't good, son. The timing couldn't be worse."

"I'm sure the dead girl agrees," I say. I hate how he always looks at the situation in response to how it affects our lives.

"I'm serious, Ben."

So am I.

"With you coming front and center to the Connolly Clan and getting too close to the granddaughter—"

"Becca."

"Whatever, son. This will blow back on us. We have to sort it out. We know these woods. We know the LaRettes have pack meetings here."

"Yeah, but other than being dicks who drive too

recklessly and act like assholes, they've never done anything," I say.

"That we know of."

Becca

Grandma pulls off the gravel road along the tree line when she sees the red and blue lights flashing ahead. Three cop cars have pulled off, and one officer is already stretching tape between the trees.

She immediately heads to talk to the police as I let Morri out of the back of the SUV. She jumps down and pads up next to me.

An officer holds up his hand to keep Grandma away, but she brushes past him, tearing the police tape down. "Outta my way."

Whoa, Grandma. The officer raises his hands slightly. I cautiously pass him and shrug. He just shakes his head.

Grandma is saying something to the other officers when she waves me over. "I'm telling you, Cliff, get out of our way and let us handle this."

"Helen, I can't let you—"

"Let me? You can't let me? You know who we are."

The officer glances at me. "Helen, she's a girl—"

God, I hate that! My face gets hot and my jaw tightens.

Grandma gets right in his face. "You're damn right she is. Now, let us do our work, so we can sort this out."

He fidgets with his watch and looks around, as though seeking help.

"Cliff, we can do this one of two ways... Becca, tell Morrigan to attack."

I jerk back and look from her to the officer to her again. Is she telling me to sic my dog on a police officer? And what would that even do, anyway? She hasn't trained me to give commands. I open my mouth, but no words come out. Morri sits patiently by my side.

"Fine!" Officer Cliff says, stepping aside.

Grandma waves me to her side and takes my left arm for balance as we head down a slight incline to where the other officer is taking photos of the body.

"Gran, what would that have done? Me telling Morri to attack?" I say it quietly in case it's a trigger word.

"Nothing," she says. "But Cliff doesn't know that."

Impressive. Then I see the dead girl.

Grandma shakes her head and makes a *tsk* sound. The girl is around my age, and the only way to describe her is to say she is ripped to shreds. Her midsection is nothing but slashes doused in blood. I cover my mouth, horrified.

"Hey, you can't be here!" the officer taking photos protests, looking up the slope to his boss.

"Tell Morrigan to go," she instructs me.

"Go on, Morri. Go!" I say, waving her to the victim.

With permission to walk around freely, Morri immediately rushes to the scene of the crime and sniffs around frantically, avoiding any disruption of the girl and the scene.

"We're fine," Grandma assures the officer as she takes a closer look. "Wolves all right," she says, but her look to me says it's more than just wolves.

The officer takes his hat off and runs his hand through his hair. "Looks like."

Morri is manic, running around sniffing, and in no time

she's left the scene and follows tracks that lead deeper into the woods. Grandma breaks away and starts following her, so I tail both of them.

Ben

"You know I can't tell you anything, Ryan," the sheriff says.

"Yeah, I know. Mind if we take a look around?" Dad asks him.

The sheriff sighs and flops his arms. "Sure, why not? Everyone else is."

We don't know what that means, but Dad heads on down before the sheriff changes his mind.

I get to the body and feel the urge to vomit. I turn away. "Katie Ackerman."

"You know her, Ben?"

I nod. "She's a sophomore at Park. *Was*," I correct myself.

The officer nearby says, "We're trying to get ahold of her folks."

Dad gets down on one knee by the body for a closer look. I'm good standing where I am.

"Yeah, it's what we expected," he confirms.

My senses are heightened. I smell the metallic blood since there's so much of it. My muscles tense. It's not that I want to taste it. It's that I feel a need that must taste it. I take a few steps away.

"You okay, Ben?" Dad asks. "Get some air."

He knows, but he doesn't know. He's in denial partially. He wants my curse not to be true. He wants me to be an average kid. Intellectually he knows I'm drawn to the blood, but he doesn't comprehend the need, the twist in my gut, the flow of saliva in my mouth. I am disgusted with myself, so I head back to the truck.

If I know Dad, he looks around with his flashlight for other clues, just as the cops are doing. He'll look for tracks, too. But the forest is big. The odds of coming up on the werewolf or pack that did this is unlikely at night.

I've been to a few sightings like this before, but never with a dead person. A few times we came upon people who were injured and unconscious, so they conveniently couldn't tell what had happened to them. Something large and hairy came from the woods was all they'd been able to say. And we've looked at animal maulings before. A few cattle and a few dogs. But this is big. This is careless. This is a sign of a feral shift.

My blood runs hot in my veins. I'm going to need a cold shower when I get home and possibly some tai chi and meditation. It's a good thing Sam didn't come with us. This would set him off. I climb in the truck and try to focus on something other than blood and moonlight.

Dad heads up the bank but stops and turns around. Then I see them. Becca and Mrs. Russell come out of the trees down below by the victim where we'd just left. Dad heads back down to them. I'm torn. I want to go to Becca. I want to know what they're talking about, but I can't get close to that smell. I take deep breaths and try to compose myself. I crack the window in case I can hear what they're saying.

Dad takes Mrs. Russell's hand and helps her up the bank while Becca and the wolfhound stay down around the crime scene. Mrs. Russell stands with her hands on her hips, facing off with him, and Dad is taking a respectful posture. He's talking to her and putting his hands together, pleading. At one point, he looks to me in the truck and gestures. He's doing an awful lot of talking, and Mrs. Russell is doing an awful lot of standing with an angry face. When he finishes, she shakes her head and blurts something out at him. She then starts pointing her finger at him and shouting. This isn't going well.

She turns away and waves Becca up. Becca shades her eyes with her hand to block out the headlights aimed in her direction. She squints and I wave, though I'm not sure if she can see me in the dark. She waves with her injured, splinted hand, and I feel bad for her. I also feel drawn to her. I want to help her, protect her. I wish I'd been at Lake Pizza five minutes sooner. I could've punched Teddy and saved her hand. I know how to throw a punch. I can take Teddy LaRette for at least a few minutes before taking a dirt nap.

My body is on alert from the blood, and it switches from wanting to feed and fight, to wanting to take Becca and kiss her, throw her wildly against the truck and push my body into her. I take deep breaths again and attempt to get myself under control. Definitely a cold shower as soon as I get home.

She makes her way to their SUV ahead of us, tucks her blonde hair behind her ear, and opens the back up for Morri to jump in. She looks back at me one last time and smiles. She's lingering. She wants to come to me, and I want her to.

Dad throws open the door and gets in. "God, that woman!"

I snap out of it. I breathe and think of how cold the lake feels when you jump in after mowing in the summer sun all day. Cold, calm, controlled.

"You okay, buddy?"

I nod. "Let's just go."

"I'm sorry, if you knew the girl."

"It's a big school. I know a lot of people." Just drive. "What was that about?" I gesture to Mrs. Russell's Grand Cherokee as it drives off, taking Becca away from me.

"Nothing. Just trying to tell her what I think. Compare notes. The werewolves. They're making a move. This is a brazen act," he says.

I nod.

"I think I know the trigger."

I look at him as he starts the truck and pulls out onto the road.

"What?" I ask, but I don't want to know the answer. I already know. I already know what has changed recently. I already know what has turned our fairly dormant supernatural world to extraordinary degrees.

He glances at me. "That Connolly Clan girl."

I take a deep breath and exhale. "Her name's Becca, Dad. Becca Redford."

CHAPTER 18

Becca

We didn't stray too far into the woods before Grandma had me call Morrigan back. Then she made me stay down by the cops while she squared off with Ben's dad. I watched Ben in the truck while he looked on. He seemed tense, but who wouldn't be? A girl at his school was killed. He frowned as Grandma and his Dad talked. I could almost see him grit his teeth. I don't think he even noticed me.

"Tracking them at night isn't a good idea." Grandma leans forward as she drives. Then she points at the moon. "It's waxing. Not even yet full."

"So what was that all about?" I ask.

"We need to train you on moon phases and their effects while you're out of commission with that hand. I'll give you some books when we get home. How long does the doctor say you'll have to keep your hand splinted?"

She's avoiding the question. "Six weeks. So what was that about?"

"Well, the good news is slayers heal quickly. It's a thing. But we should ease up on physical training anyway. We can have you work on command words with Morrigan. She's ready."

"Gran!"

"Oh, all right, Becca! Ryan Hunt has an interest in these killings, probably because of how werewolves tie into his family. He was filling me in on his thoughts."

"Which were…"

"He knows you're a slayer," she tells me.

This freaks me out. "What? Why? How?"

"Becca, our Clan is well known in the slaying world. The Hunts take a peripheral interest in that. We're sort of legendary, to say the least. That a new slayer is being trained is huge."

I frown. I'm not sure I'm excited about that.

"And since his boys have been sniffing around you, probably literally, they have come to certain conclusions."

I'm really not excited about this. Frankly, if Ben has come to any conclusions about me other than I'm hot and he wants to make out at some point, I'm not sure I want to know about them. "Like what?"

"Becca, when you hit Teddy LaRette… Describe that for me."

"What do you mean?"

She turns to me. "What made you go from thinking this guy is a jerk to thinking you had to punch him? What went through your head?"

I take a deep breath and try to remember. I explain the rage I felt and the irrational need to hurt that total dick. I tell her how the fury came from every cell in my body and into my fist, and all I knew was total anger and a desire to destroy.

"Have you felt that way before?" she asks.

I think for a minute. "Maybe when it's that time of the month sometimes, but not really to that extent."

"Have you felt that way around Ben or his brothers?"

"What? No, God, Gran!"

She nods and sighs. "Maybe I'm wrong about them, and Ryan is right. Maybe you are a sister of the moon, and my training regimen hasn't been right for you at all."

Oh good. More weird shit that I don't understand. "A sister of the moon?"

Grandma tells me that sisters of the moon are pretty much slayers on steroids. Most slayers simply have it in their blood to handle their wolfhound but have no real powers or abilities of their own. Sisters of the moon are typically born on nights of full moons, are destined to be slayers, and take on certain extra abilities. They think I can sense werewolves because the LaRettes have been on Grandma's radar, and apparently the Hunt's radar, for some time.

The next phase of my training includes Gran giving me books to read. I'm not big on reading, but I take them outside and listen to my favorite tunes while I peruse them. David Bowie, Prince, Marshall Crenshaw, The Cure. I'm not sure how I got into 80s music. I mean Mom listens to it from time to time, but I just like it. It seems upbeat and catchy most of the time. Happy. Different.

I learn about the moon phases and their supposed effects on werewolves. Grandma also explains that there seems to be a werewolf uprising. I haven't seen one yet, unless that Teddy douche is in fact one, but I'll take her word for it.

Grandma says I should keep up my physical training, well, what I can with my hand and all, and practice with weapons, but she shifts focus. She starts teaching me meditation and opening my mind. She says sisters of the moon, like wolfhounds, work on instinct, so I need to clear my mind of all blockages so I can tap into that.

Blockages. Like my parents' impending divorce. Mom got the papers a few days after the murder, and cried for two days. Apparently Dad has a new girlfriend. Gross. I'm sad for Mom. I stop responding to Dad's texts.

The murder investigation is full on, but the sheriff's department is on the wrong track. When my hand is somewhat better, Grandma says we should scout the woods. She says I'm as ready as I'll ever be, and that the only training left is for me to encounter some actual werewolves to kill. This makes me nervous. Part of me still hopes this werewolf thing is all a joke or their imagination.

I've never killed anything. I rescue spiders and bees when they get in the house and safely carry them outside. But Grandma says it will be instinct, and I have to listen to my first bit of intuition. If I don't, I could die. Thanks for that, Gran.

Grandma goes to her room and comes out with a green velvet jewelry box. She takes out a flat, mint green stone on a chain and hands it to me. "Here, wear this."

"That's beautiful, Gran. Thank you!"

"It is beautiful, but it's also powerful. It glows if werewolves are around."

"What?" More shit I can't believe.

"It's a moonstone necklace, handed down through our family for generations. From slayer to slayer. It's yours now," she says.

"I don't know what to say."

"It only makes you aware of werewolves in your presence. It doesn't protect you, so don't rely on it too much."

I wear it from then on.

I go to Lake Pizza a few more times and chat with Maddie, who is fascinated by me now. She gets me free Diet Cokes every time I go in and reports that Teddy hasn't bothered her since. When it's not busy, I sit at the counter, and Maddie gives me the scoop on Park High.

"It's pretty cool as far as high school goes, I guess. The teachers are okay. Well, there was one last year who was arrested for killing a bunch of students. She set off a bomb. It was weird," she tells me.

My eyebrows shoot up. "Yeah, that sounds weird." Understatement of the year. "A teacher killed a bunch of students by bombing the school?"

"She was involved in some Satanic cult. I can't remember how many students were killed—over a hundred, but they've rebuilt the part that was blown up since. It should be finished by the time we start back."

I remember hearing about this on the news now that she mentions it. "That's crazy." Satanic cult...my mind goes right to the demonic curse that causes lycanthropy and wonders if there is a connection.

"Other than her, the teachers are nice. Students are pretty cool. There are some cute guys. What more can you want?" she says, then someone comes up to order.

The place sounds bizarre, but from what I've learned from Grandma about werewolves and curses, they tend to center around areas of supernatural hyperactivity. It sounds like Park High and the national forest are those types of spawn points.

"But you like Ben, right?" she says after finishing with her customer.

"What?"

"You like Ben Hunt? He was in here when you punched Teddy."

"Oh, yeah. Umm, I've met him a few times. Seems nice."

"They're all cute. The Hunt brothers. That Nic is dreamy."

I nod.

"You should go out with Ben. You'd be a cute couple," she says as she wipes down the counter.

"Okay, well, I'll let him know." I smile. No way in hell am I letting him know.

She gets a mischievous grin on her face. "Now might be a good time." And she makes herself scarce.

Ben comes up and sits on the stool next to me. "Hey, slugger," he says, and blood rushes to my face. "How's the hand?"

"Oh, this old thing?" I raise my hand that's just wrapped now. "Getting there." I scramble for something to say. "Maddie was just telling me about Park High."

"Oh, right, you'll be going there with us. Hey, Maddie, when do we register?" he shouts back to the kitchen.

He's dreamy. His eyes are super blue, his face is tanned from the summer sun, and his hair has lightened since I first saw him at the beginning of the season.

She comes out. "Now, I think. Pretty sure registration started this week."

Part of me looks forward to school. Part of me dreads it.

"We should go get our classes," Ben says. "What are you doing now?"

"Right now?"

He shrugs. "If you're busy, another time."

"She's not busy," Maddie interrupts, smirking at me.

I give her a death daggers look.

"Don't you want your schedule?" he asks.

"Yeah," Maddie adds. "Maybe we'll all have classes together." She flashes me a knowing look and juts her head toward Ben in an effort to nudge me to action.

She's going to do something to embarrass me in front of him, so maybe it's a good time to leave. "Sure, let's go." I smile and grab my purse.

Then I'm in his truck again. I feel like this means something for some reason. Like he's invited me into his territory and is showing me things about himself. The music he likes, the things hanging from his rearview mirror.

The truck is an older Ranger, but he has a new stereo in it. He swipes on his phone a few times then turns on the radio. David Bowie plays "Rebel, Rebel."

"What? You like David Bowie?" My voice comes out a high-pitched squeak. I'm in shock.

He grins but keeps his eyes on the road. "What's not to like?"

"Wow, that's so…. I love Bowie." The smile on my face is so huge I feel like a freak show, but I can't seem to get it off.

He keeps smiling. I quit talking for fear of saying something stupid.

"So how's it going at your grandmother's?" he asks.

I think we're avoiding the elephant in the truck. From what Grandma said, he knows about werewolves and he knows about me. I know something is off about his family, but I'm not sure what. But we're not talking about werewolves. We're talking about normal stuff. Maybe Grandma has it wrong. Maybe she wants me to make a fool of myself in front of him by blurting out something dumb about werewolves.

"Oh, good. It's pretty quiet really."

"Yeah?"

"How about you? How's your summer going?" I ask. Maybe he'll say something to clue me in.

"Pretty quiet, too. Mowing lawns, playing baseball, getting in the lake when I can."

"Nice." Neither one of us are going to say anything.

We small talk the rest of the way. I head into yet another new school, but they all have the same bones. Painted cement block walls, rows of lockers, idiotic posters about saying no to all sorts of appealing things, and glassed-in offices.

We get our schedules and find we have one class together. I guess it's better than nothing.

"LA 4 with Potter. He's cool. You'll like him."

"Uhhhh." I make a cringey face. "Probably not. I don't get along much with teachers."

He gives me a tour and shows me the junior lockers. He shows me the gym, like I care about gym. And he goes down to check out the reconstruction from the bomb incident Maddie had mentioned.

"Wow, most kids would be happy their school was bombed," I say.

He sighs heavily. "People died. So not really."

Way to go, Becca. Make a joke about a bunch of his classmates getting exploded.

"I'm sorry."

"It's okay. It's weird. Lots of weird things happen at this school." He has a faraway look.

"I heard," I say.

He shakes it off. "All right, I'll get you back home."

Nope. Chat killer.

I keep my damn trap shut the rest of the way, but he plays David Bowie again, so it can't be all bad.

"Becca, there's a dance this weekend. It's a community dance but they have it at the school," he says.

"Yeah?" Yay! He's asking me out! I try to be cool.

"You should go."

Blink. That's not an invitation.

"Yeah?" I ask again with less enthusiasm.

"Yeah, you could meet some people from school."

What the hell? Is he trying to hook me up?

"Okay, yeah, maybe. Are you going?"

"Probably. Yeah, I think."

"Okay. Maybe."

He stops in front of my house.

"Thanks," I say and hold up my schedule.

"No problem." He smiles politely and turns the radio down.

"Bye." I get out and give him a half-hearted wave.

He drives off.

What the F was that? My bomb joke went over with a bang, and not in a good bomb bang kind of way. Oh well. I fucked that up. Maybe it's for the best. I didn't get an inkling that he knew about werewolves or wanted to talk about them. Grandma is off her rocker. And my necklace didn't glow or anything.

At least she won't have to worry about me and Ben hooking up anymore. He is clearly not interested in me.

Ben

Oh my God, I love her. The way she smiles when I play Bowie. I remember the shirt she was wearing the first time I saw her the night Teddy LaRette almost ran her over. She wore an old David Bowie Glass Spiders tour concert T-shirt. She lights up when I turn Bowie on. And she's always thinking and keeps her cards close to her chest. I know she knows all about werewolves, but she doesn't give any clues to that. I don't know if she knows that I know. I don't know what her grandmother has told her about us. I don't know how my bloodline will affect us. I don't know what all she knows, and I don't want to be the one to blurt it all out to her.

But God, she's gorgeous, and a sister of the moon, Nic and Dad think. How amazing is that?

We found out we have a class together! I wish we had more. Maybe I could rearrange a few things. Is that stalkery?

I want to tell her everything. I want to tell her how my mom was turned when she was pregnant with me. I want to explain that I can control it, that I'm not a full werewolf, that I am stronger than lycanthropy, that I am stronger than the pull of the moon. But I'm not sure how true that last part is. I'm not sure what she would do.

I hate it. I hate the curse. I'm ashamed that I have this hunger in me. I always have been.

My mind is whirring. I tell her about the dance, but it comes out all wrong. I tell her to go. I don't ask her to go with me. I'm an idiot, but I'm trying to remember what to tell Dad. Where we should maybe start investigating on this murder. Katie's murder.

Dad's construction company has been working on part of the reconstruction of the school. I showed Becca, and though I remember some of the people who died, I start to wonder. Lycanthropy is caused by a demonic curse. Last year the news covered a little bit about the bomb and shared that some strange runes had been left in the boiler room and in the theater. The theory was that Mrs. McNair was Satanic, so she killed to appease the devil. Major whack job. But I wonder how much of that Dad checked out. I'm thinking it could be a spawn point. The bomb was placed in the boiler room. I wonder how much evidence survived.

I'd planned on asking Becca to the dance, but my mind goes foggy trying to figure things out. So many died last year. One has already died this year. How many more will die before we figure out where the packs are, who is leading them, and why they are making themselves known?

Dad could easily get down there and have a look. Though so could I. I go to school here. I wonder if we should go back. I could take Becca. Maybe I could see what she can do.... Slayer wise, of course. I wasn't thinking about what she could do otherwise. I get distracted and start wondering if she's a good kisser.

Dammit, Ben. Get it together. I drop her off, and all I can think about is kissing her and how badly I screwed up that date thing. I don't even know if she's going now. She makes me nervous, and my head is all over the place.

I really like that girl. She cusses, she listens to retro music, and she runs. She doesn't like teachers. She punches dirtbags. She is fearless. I really like her, and I can't stop wondering if she would like me, too, or if she would just want to kill me.

CHAPTER 19

Becca

"Becca, I think this is a bad idea," Grandma tells me as I walk out the kitchen door anyway. "You really haven't spent enough time bonding with Morrigan. You've been too busy with this boy. Have you even read the books I gave you? And you wanted information on the spell..."

"I'm going to the dance, Gran. Tell Mom I'll be home by midnight...ish." I put earbuds in and walk through the woods to the high school.

Morri peeks out the front window, her ears to the side. Grandma is right. I haven't spent enough time with her. Oh well. I also haven't seen any werewolves to speak of, so I'm kinda done playing monster killer. Right now, I'm more into playing hot guy killer, I mean stalker, specifically Ben.

I don't get far before Grandma drives up beside me and hands me my crossbow. "If you're going, at least take this." Morri peeks out from the back window.

125

"Where am I supposed to put that? Like they'll let me walk into the school with a crossbow?"

"Stash it outside. Stick it under your shirt. I don't care, but take it," she says, continuing to thrust it in my direction.

I do the classic eye roll/heavy sigh maneuver, perfected by teenage girls since the dawn of time. "Fine! But I'm not taking her!" I jut my finger at Morrigan who looks dejected for a moment.

Grandma sees my classic teen girl eye roll and raises me an I'm-too-old-for-this-crap eye roll back before driving off.

The school is a seven-minute drive, but who's counting. I can, however, cut through the woods and walk there in twenty or so, and this way, I can ask Ben for a ride home. I have it all worked out. And if he isn't there or is with another girl or for whatever reason can't give me a ride home, Maddie said she'll be there, and I'll catch a ride with her.

I'm sort of shocked that I actually like it here. I was dreading the move at the beginning of summer, dreading another new school, and dreading my parents separating. Lots of dread was going on. But it's been nice getting to know Grandma. And it's been nice meeting some other people and hanging out on the lake. I usually am not into other people, but Ben and Maddie seem like good people. They get my mind off the other stuff.

I've never started a new school where I knew some of the people going into it. I'm actually looking forward to that.

Maybe I shouldn't hit on Ben. What if it blows up in my face? Then the only person I'll know without awkwardness is Maddie. I'm not sure that I can't hit on Ben. I mean, I feel like I have to. Like I have no control. I know it's stupid. I know love is stupid. I know relationships and all that are a load of crap. But a girl wants what a girl wants.

I turn on the flashlight on my phone to see the path through the woods. Yes, the path through the woods where the murdered girl was found. These are big woods. I'm just cutting through. I won't be here long. But yeah, these are the woods they said you shouldn't walk through, during the day, let alone at night.

Oh well. Bring on the werewolves. At least I'll see one finally. I glance at the moon. Contrary to what Gran thinks, I've read the boring books. I know about the moon and the training and the history and the dog stuff. I know about the kill points and weaknesses of the werewolves. I know all the gory details about all of it. I just need to put it into practice somehow.

It's a half moon. That tells me absolutely nothing. Things with werewolves can go either way. Is it half full or half empty? I'm gonna say half full, which in this case makes me a pessimist. Half full regarding werewolves means they could be turned, worked into a frenzy, and on the prowl. Yeah, pessimist seems about right. Though I did pack my trusty dagger, Stabby McStabberson, in my woven bucket purse. I don't know that they do weapons checks before school dances here or not. Knowing the history of Park High, they probably should.

I wore my calf-length boyfriend jeans, though they didn't belong to any boy I know, and if they did, he'd be kind of girly. I guess that's okay. And I wore a tank top with a button-down shirt over it with the moonstone necklace Gran gave me. I wore my hair up and put on some lipstick. I haven't worn makeup most of the summer unless I was heading to the pizza place hoping to see Ben, but tonight I'm dressing to impress. I hope, anyway.

I find myself humming that tune again. *Who's afraid of the big, bad wolf?* I pop in my earbuds and turn on my music to get it out of my head. I pick some Prince and Duran Duran on my walk. They'll probably play pop garbage tonight, but I'm not going to the dance to actually dance. That's too mainstream.

In no time, it seems, I arrive at the school. I hold my crossbow discreetly at my side as I make my way for some bushes by the front door. It should be safe there. Then I head for the gym.

Since I was there earlier this week, the pep club or whatever the hell they call it, has decorated the gym in a summer beach theme. Pep Club. Who the hell would join that? Like I want to be peppy? Ugh, gross. The music is pounding already, and people are milling around the doors, sneaking smokes out front.

I push past them and follow the sounds to the dance. I scan the gym through the flashing lights to find my two friends. I spot Ben first, standing off by the bleachers with a red Solo cup in his hand. He's leaning against the wall talking to someone I don't know, gesturing with his drink-holding hand. He looks so casual and relaxed. So gorgeous and hot.

What is my ever-loving deal? Snap out of it, Becca. Get a grip. I look away and pretend I don't see him in case he looks at me. I can't be the one to make contact first. Where is Maddie?

At that, Maddie pounces up behind me. I nearly leap to the ceiling and cling to it like a scared cartoon cat, but I remain on the gym floor. I put my hand to my slamming heart. "You scared the life out of me."

Maddie is dressed for the dance. She has a brown and blue ponytail and dark, geek-chic glasses, torn skinny jeans, a Deadpool T-shirt, and several rubber bracelets with comic symbols on them. She gives me an encouraging smile.

"He's over theeeeerrre," she says in a sing-songy voice, pointing right at him.

"Oh?" I turn the opposite way and face her. "I didn't notice." I will her to be cool on my behalf.

"Let me introduce you to some people. We'll see if he comes to you. That's always a good sign," she advises me. "We'll make sure you're available. Don't go to him first. You'll tip your hand."

"Good to know."

High school is stupid. School dances are stupid. I guess, ergo, by argument, you could say that I'm stupid, since I'm the one at the dance at my soon-to-be brand new, shiny high school. Haven't even started here yet and already I'm among the misguided idiots who come to dances looking for love, of all things.

I cross my arms over my chest, as though to shield me from the embarrassment of approaching the other losers who came to the dance.

Three students are sitting at a table that Maddie walks me up to. "Hey, guys," she shouts over the pounding music, "this is Becca Russell. She'll be starting here next month."

"Redford," I correct her, but too soft for anyone to actually catch.

A chorus of hellos and how are yous ensue.

But why bother? I doubt I'll be at this school next year. Hell, I may not be here next month. From what I hear, that Park High even still stands is a miracle in and of itself.

A semi-cute guy, also with glasses, is sitting there, reading his phone. He looks up and nods. "Hi. I'd tell you my name, but you won't remember it," he says over the music and goes back to his phone.

Another girl with long blonde hair shaved a few inches over her right ear is at the table. She sports a well-worn, black, studded leather jacket, leather skinny jeans, biker boots, and black—mostly chipped off—nail polish. "Hey." She doesn't look like she cares enough to even tell me her name.

I'm hating this meeting-new-people thing. I glance over to the wall where I'd last seen Ben. He glances over at me and flashes a brief smile in acknowledgment before turning back to his buddy. I swoon a little. My mind wanders to his smile and his low, sexy voice. I size him up from a safe distance. His hair is sandy blond, a little wavy on top, but he's clean-cut, varsity jacket all the way. Perfect teeth, perfect smile, perfect hands. Why am I staring at his hands? My attraction for him is stupid, I decide. Stupid like me.

After all, I'll never be a normal high school girl. I shouldn't even be here. I'll never have sleepovers, go to movies, or date anyone, ever, at all again. My heart breaks a little. Nothing like that for me. I can't do normal now. I wish I could, but I'm not normal. I'm cursed.

My grandma would say "gifted." I've learned there is a very fine line between gifted and cursed. There is no way in hell being chosen to be a werewolf slayer is a gift. Grandma was or is a slayer, and it runs in the family. Unfortunately for me, it landed squarely on my shoulders. And so we're here. Apparently in the middle of a local influx of werewolves just in time to find out I'm a slayer and have to fight them.

And maybe die.

But not date, swoon, dance, make the honor roll. Those

things are a low priority. Make that no priority. Not that I'd make the honor roll anyway. Though it'd be nice to think I could.

I gaze longingly at Ben. My heart beats faster. Like who would want to date a werewolf slayer anyway?

I don't know much about dating, but I can tell you a little something about training wolfhounds. That's pretty much it. Which makes me a horrible conversationalist with others my age.

I pry my gaze away from Ben to check out who else is in the room. Maddie is staring at me, giving me an encouraging look.

"What?"

A few of the other students glance over at me. I wonder what their assessment of me is. I'm clean, I guess. I'm cute. I have blondish hair. My hair is up in a messy bun that took me thirty minutes to do, so it'd seem like it took thirty seconds. My hand is still wrapped, but healing quickly.

I glance out the window. A brief pang of homesickness strikes me, but I'm not sick for home exactly. I miss my dog. For some reason, I start to regret not spending more time with her. I've been avoiding this slayer thing to hang out or look for Ben.

It sounds stupid, but Morrigan is special. She chose me. She bonded with me. I don't know why or how or whatever, but she did, and now the family legacy, the curse, the burden we carry is on my shoulders. Yeah, because my dog loves me. It's weird, I know.

Ugh, ugh, ugh. I have an intense desire to bail.

Ben

Here I am again, but this time, it isn't the usual suspects. Typically these summer dances at the school are just the people who have nothing better to do than go. But this time, Becca is here.

She walks in. I lean casually on the stacked bleachers and look away immediately, hoping she didn't catch me notice. I should go to her. I was supposed to ask her to this thing. But Jack is going on and on about football tryouts and team captain, so I feel like I can't leave him. I also don't want to jump on her when she first walks in. Not jump on her like that, but then there's that, too.

She's gorgeous. Blonde-streaked hair thrown up on her head. Dark eyes, a chain around her neck with a stone pendant on the end. Bangles on her wrists. I can't explain it. I'm drawn to something about her. Jack fades into the background, and I no longer have any clue what he's saying.

She stands tall, walks in quickly, and Maddie leads her away to her table of friends, which is not too far from me, but yet too far.

Dude, what is wrong with me? Pull yourself together. It doesn't matter who she is or how she looks. She is not for me. I can't date her. Dad is right. She's a Connolly. She is training to kill people like me. She can't know my secret. To the rest of the world, I play the varsity-football-guy role to blend in. Others don't get to know me. Me is weird.

Becca and I haven't even really talked. I don't know who she is. She doesn't know who I am. I don't like talking to girls. I don't like small talk. Jack drones on. I don't even like talking about football. I want to talk about something real. I want to talk about what a girl wants and what I want. I want to hear her hopes and her dreams and tell her mine. I want to discuss the meaning of life. I want to know what she thinks about the struggle of good vs. evil. Can someone be entirely good? Can someone find a balance in between? Is there a middle ground? I want to know what she thinks, because I don't have the answers to these things.

I've seen evil. I've stared it in the face. I've stood toe-to-toe with a monster as it exhaled its hot, stale breath on me. And I've seen it in the eyes of my own mother.

I've seen those who fight against evil. Does that mean they are good? When I look in the mirror, do I see my dad's goodness or my mom's darkness looking back at me? Once again, I hate what I am.

I shake my head. I've asked girls questions like this before. What is the meaning of life? They look at me like I'm nuts. And maybe I am. I'd just like to connect with someone.

I can't *not* look at her. I glance her way. Our eyes meet. I smile and turn away. It's cute. It's like we had a moment. Get over it!

It's ridiculous. But God, she's beautiful. She looks around at everyone, taking us all in. The music thrums and the lights swirl around, so I get clear views of her off and on until the light flashes in another direction. She's curious. She's deep in thought. I wonder what she's thinking. I wonder what she wants. I wonder what she loves in this world. Is she looking for me?

It's pointless. Focus, Ben. Pull your crap together. Play the part. Do your job. Don't let yourself be distracted. Keep your eye on the big picture. People are dying. Don't be distracted by Becca Redford, and if she is the slayer, a sister of the moon, then don't get in her way.

CHAPTER 20

Becca

Ben glances over at me. I blush like a fucking idiot.

"So?" Maddie's eyebrows shoot up, waiting expectantly for my answer.

"What?" I have no idea what she just asked me. My brain is all over the place. Or maybe it's my heart. Either way, I'm clueless.

"That's Abigail," Maddie tells me. "Abby Mason."

"Abby," I repeat loudly, like a trained parrot.

"What do you want, cupcake?" she asks me.

I frown.

"I'm Kyle," the guy says, I guess deciding I'll remember now.

"He's a straight-A brainiac." Maddie says, all smiles.

"Yeah, his parents have the honor roll bumper sticker to prove it," Abby adds.

"Great! Now everyone knows everyone," Maddie says.

The others continue to shout to each other over the music. The lights are starting to give me a headache.

And then my moonstone necklace glows. I've never seen it glow before, partly because I rarely wear it, but also because it's only supposed to glow when werewolves are around. I clutch it to hide the glowing. I wouldn't know how to explain it. Luckily the crazy DJ lights are keeping it from being that noticeable. But I notice. And I have no idea what to do. My mind immediately goes to Morrigan like an instinct.

"Shit," I say aloud.

The others stop and eye me.

"Did you say something?" Maddie asks, turning to me.

My moonstone glows brighter. I can now see it through my fingers.

"Shit, shit, shit." I assess my wardrobe and frantically go through my purse. Had I brought anything in case of a werewolf emergency? Of course not. Not that I should beat myself up too much. I've never had a fucking werewolf emergency before. Oh, there's Stabby McStabberson! My stomach tightens, and I start to tremble. This is my first, and I'm nervous as fuck. And my hand starts to hurt just from going through my purse.

"What is your deal?" Abby asks.

"I have to go. I have to go get something." I've gotta get my bow. I suddenly wish I'd brought Morrigan. I'm so fucked.

"What's going on?" Ben asks. "What kind of necklace is that?"

I hadn't seen him walk up to me. How long has he been standing there? Doesn't matter. He just drew attention to my necklace, so now they all notice.

"Cool! A rave necklace?" Abby says, standing up and leaning in to get a better view. "How does that work?"

"I gotta go."

"Go? Go where? You just got here. I was hoping to...dance with you," Ben says, sort of slowly at the end like he didn't want to finish his sentence.

I stop, and a small burst of butterflies explodes in my core. "You did?"

His face goes red. Or maybe it's the disco lights.

I stand there, momentarily waiting, forgetting danger is approaching, forgetting something very weird is about to happen. A bark jolts me to my senses. What the hell? Do werewolves bark? I don't know anything about them or what they do, or how they fight except for what Grandma has told me or what I've read in books, and my brain seems to have forgotten all of it at this moment.

Ben straightens at the sound of the bark. A bark so loud it sounded over the short break in the music. "What the hell?" He looks around for the source.

"I have to go!" I grab my purse, rush out of the gym, and hang a right down the hall.

"Wait!" Ben shouts after me.

"Becca!" Maddie calls out, too.

Shit, they'll be hurt by the werewolf. I run down the hall. I have to do something. I have a burning desire to do something.

I hurry to the front doors and snatch my crossbow from the bushes. Six bolts are in the attached quiver. Better make 'em count, but I'm hoping I won't need to. I strap Stabby McStabberson to my thigh and hoist the crossbow on my right side. Great. Weapons at a school function. I may as well prepare to be expelled. And school hasn't even started yet. Great, I'll just go to jail.

I can sense Morrigan somehow. Is she coming? How did she know? How does any of this work? How will I explain a 140-pound dog running up to me in the middle of the dance? Psssht, I'll worry about that later.

I rush back through the front doors. Behind me, a loud bark sounds. I pause and turn, stepping aside with the door open just in time for her to burst in, ears flying behind her, long teeth bared, eyes narrowed. Normally she's so sweet and derpy, but in werewolf-hunting mode, she looks positively terrifying.

She skids in. The frequently waxed floor does no favors for her big, clawed feet. She does a Bambi on ice impression as she gains her footing.

"Easy, Morri," I say.

She calms slightly and her nose lifts as she inhales for the trace. She looks like some sort of African war dog, with her gray and tan stripes. Her head hits me just below my chest area. Her ears are long and flop over, but they're peaked, angled out at the sides. She's looking. She's a sight hound, a supernatural one at that. She can sense werewolves miles away.

"You'd better be sure about this werewolf thing. If you out me or get me expelled—" My necklace is glowing like mad. There's a werewolf nearby, or Morri and the moonstone are both off.

My heart pounds, and adrenaline surges through my body. A low growl ripples through Morri as she glares to her right, toward the gym. Crap, that's where I just was. That's where a bunch of innocent students are dancing and having fun. Of course, my first threat would be in the most highly visible place in the school on a Saturday night. Couldn't possibly be in the middle of the forest, alone. I've got to fight a werewolf, explain it all, and have everyone watching my first time, too.

Morri races to the gym, me behind her trying to keep up.

"Becca?" Maddie asks. All of them—Ben, Maddie, Abby, and Kyle—are standing at the gym doors staring at me. "What are you doing with that dog? And that weapon?"

Morri stares at the gym doors. She wants in so bad, she's shaking.

"Listen, you have to get out of here. I can't explain—"

Screams erupt from the gym.

"Now!"

"I'm coming with you," Ben says to me.

"Are you crazy?" Kyle asks.

"You can't—" I start to argue with him, but Morri's ears are straight back, and her teeth are bared. "Do what you want."

I hope I don't get everyone killed, especially myself.

Ben

We're having a moment. Our eyes meet. Becca's happy I wanted to dance with her. I think. Or shocked. Or disgusted. I really am not great at interpreting girl reactions. Not that it matters. But before I can figure out what's happening, something sets her off. She starts swearing and going through her things, and I sense something, too, but can't keep my eyes off her. Then she says she has to go, and out she bolts, tearing down the hall.

"What is with her?" Abby asks, the music still blaring in the background.

Kyle shakes his head.

"I've got a bad feeling about this," I say, which causes Maddie to burst out laughing for some reason.

"Nothing, it's a *Star Wars* thing—never mind," she says.

Will I need my gear? Is it that bad? I get a whiff of something that seems off. I can't keep my eyes off Becca. I jog out of the gym after her to see where she's heading. She runs to the front of the school. I glance over to the empty locker I threw my stuff in.

The others follow me and plug the doorway to the gym, looking around. They have no clue what could be happening.

I creep to my locker and take out my blade. I slip it inside my jacket, unseen, and return to the others who still huddle at the double doors. Becca reappears with her dog. She stops nearby, and the wolfhound starts growling, eyeing me, then eyeing the doors to the gym.

Becca orders us to leave when screams come from the gym behind us. I know exactly what's going on. She really is what my brother and my dad thought. But has she fought werewolves before?

I start after her. "I'm coming with you!"

CHAPTER 21

Becca

I slam the gym doors open so hard they bang against the wall. Morri is off like a racehorse, and about the same size. Inside, the music is still blaring and the lights are all crazy, so it's hard to focus. Most of the student body is headed toward one of three exits, one being the doorway I'm standing in. I leap to the side, and Morri navigates her way through them.

Students are screaming and running out. They scream louder at Morri and avoid her. If they saw werewolves inside, they probably think she's one, too.

Students are hemorrhaging from the gym in all directions. Pretty fast, too. The opposite side has cleared out, leaving me a view of my very first werewolf. It's got three poor students cornered at the far end of the court.

It stands about seven feet tall, and it looks like an enormous wolf walking on two legs with forepaws reaching out like hands. The head is larger and the snout, too.

My jaw drops and my eyes are wide. I'm shocked, but not so shocked either. Grandma has prepared me for this. I was skeptical but also knew it was coming. How is it possible? I don't know, but it is in this world. In my new normal. My moonstone necklace glows.

Morri waits beside me, shaking, as the creature snarls and creeps toward its prey. From my peripheral vision, two other students scurry up across the stands to escape. Morri's bark echoes through the gym, amplifying it, even over the music. The DJ has left the building, so the when the current song ends, the music is over, though the lights continue to dance.

The werewolf turns our direction. It has a full-court length to travel to attack us, but so does Morri to attack it. I raise and level my crossbow, aiming between its eyes, though the twirling lights make it hard to aim.

"Why don't you pick on someone your own size?" I ask, then wish I'd taken more time to compose my taunts because that's stupid.

The beast stands upright. It growls and eyes us, giving the students enough time to make a run for it, through the gym door at the opposite side of the room. The other two climb down the bleachers behind me and run out the doors I came in.

"Thanks for your help," I call out.

The room is clear now except for the monster, me, and my wolfhound.

Before I can wonder about it too long, the werewolf breaks into a run on all fours at us.

I let a bolt fly in its direction, but it zings past as the beast bears down in a gallop. Shit. And ow, it hurts my hand.

Morri takes her cue. She tries to find her footing on the waxed court and scrambles awkwardly for purchase before launching herself at the werewolf. Luckily there's only one.

Growling sounds behind me. I turn to see another werewolf coming out from under the bleachers, as though it had been hiding. That seems oddly strategic.

I reload and aim while Morri and the werewolf snarl and scuffle behind me. A tinge of worry hits me, but I need to focus on my monster. That's the deal. She can handle hers, and I try to handle mine. My werewolf approaches me slowly, cautiously, stalking its prey.

Bolt in, level my aim, pull the trigger, feel the pain in my hand, and let the bolt fly, all in one smooth motion that takes only a few seconds. The good news is he's only a dozen feet away. I can hit him. The bad news is he's only a dozen feet away, so he's gonna come at me if I don't drop him.

The bolt bites deep into its shoulder. It yelps in pain. Yay, I hit it. Boo, it's only the shoulder, so he doesn't go down. I steel myself against any fear, and robotically pluck another bolt from my quiver and pull back the string.

He turns and comes at me. My hand is shaking too much for me to get the damn bolt in and pull back. Morri is too far away. I can't possibly make another shot before he hits me.

Behind me, a sharp yelp is followed by a sickening crack. Then the sound of nails hitting the court floor and heading towards me. I'm sure it is Morri. I can feel her, coming to take care of my monster, though she has a basketball court to cover to get to me.

My monster lunges for me, and I'm not even near ready to let another bolt go. I brace for impact, but it yelps and falls to the ground two feet in front of me in a lump, twitching. How did that happen?

Ben is standing where the werewolf had been, gripping a hunting knife hilt coated in blood. Morri is immediately at my side, whimpering excitedly.

"Are you okay?" Ben asks. He rushes over to me, his brows furrowed. He looks calm like it was nothing, like he just took out the trash.

I blink and stand there dumbfounded. What just happened?

"Becca, are you okay?" He lays a hand on my arm. Morri growls, so Ben takes his hand away and holds it up in surrender.

"Am I okay? Are *you* okay?"

He laughs. "I'm fine. And that's two, by the way."

"Two?"

"Two times I've saved you. If you're keeping score."

Morri gives him a hard look. She glances at his blade and cautiously walks to him and sniffs at it, then backs away, looking from him to the dead werewolf crumpled on the floor. Odd, but I'm kind of confused now, too.

I check her over for injuries, and she seems fine. The only blood on her is around her muzzle. I glance back at her werewolf who is more a pile of blood and guts than a werewolf now. I check on mine, or should I say Ben's? The monster lies still. Blood runs out of its side.

"You're okay, then?" Ben asks.

He scans the room. I do the same, making sure no other monsters are lurking around. The dance lights are still flashing and spinning without music to guide them.

"So, you're a werewolf slayer after all?" Ben takes a cloth out of his varsity jacket and wipes his weapon clean. It's a long, curved hunting knife with runes engraved along the blade. He sheathes it, folds the cloth up, and puts it back in his pocket as he grins at me.

"Ummmm, yeah. You?"

He laughs. "Yup. Well, I'm a werewolf...uhhh hunter I guess. Know a few things about hunting werewolves. My dad tracks them, so. And you are the new slayer for the Connolly Clan."

"Oh, uh, yeah." I literally shake my head to snap out of it. How bizarre is it, having a conversation like this with a guy from school? A cute guy from school. A cute guy from school with dreamy eyes... "My grandmother's clan... Yeah, anyway."

He stares at me a second, then responds with, "Cool."

"What the ever-loving fuck?" Abby asks, entering the gym and seeing two gruesome piles of mutilated beast on the gym floor.

"Wild animal attack?" I flash a half-hearted smile.

Kyle and Maddie trail in behind her. "What happened here?" Kyle asks. Maddie just stares, eyes wide.

I open my mouth to respond, not knowing what to say when Ben takes over.

"It's a long story, guys," he says. "Let's get out of here, and I'll explain it."

"What, and we're supposed to leave this here?" I ask him.

He shrugs. "No one saw us here. We leave it, we don't have to explain it."

"Well, yeah, people saw me come in, crossbow blazing."

Ben exhales and puts his hands on his hips. "Wild animals broke in. That's the usual story. People around here are in denial and like it that way."

"And I just happened to have weapons and a hunting dog with me?" I counter.

Morri licks my hand on cue. There's no explaining this.

Ben locks eyes with me. "There's never a way to explain this, Becca.

Kyle steps forward. "Wild animals? These aren't any animals I've ever seen."

"No way!" Maddie says, getting a closer look at the one on the floor by us. "That's a werewolf!"

"Excuse me? Have you lost your mind, Maddie?" Kyle asks.

"Look at it! I've heard rumors about werewolves in the woods. And then after what happened with Katie…"

"You can't be… Are you serious?" Kyle asks, then walks around the creature and eyes it closer, his hand on his chin.

Ben and I don't say anything. We look at each other and wait.

Abby runs up to examine it now, too. "It's no wolf. You have to admit that."

Kyle shakes his head. "This is crazy. This…this…" He looks Ben and I up and down. Me with my crossbow and my bloodied hunting dog. "These are werewolves, and you're both werewolf hunters?"

"She's a slayer if you want to get technical. I'm a hunter," Ben says.

Blank stares answer him, including mine.

"Slayers are typically solo. Hunters work in teams.

"All righty then. Let's just get out of here." Kyle heads out the gym doors as though nothing happened.

Abby stares at me, then at Ben, then follows Kyle.

"We should go. I should get Morri home and check in with Gran."

"You sure you're good?" Ben asks.

"I'm good." I force a smile.

"So there really are werewolves and werewolf hunters at our school?" Maddie turns to us.

Ben looks at me. There's no denying it at this point. "Yes."

"That is so friggin' cool." A smile spreads across her face.

Sirens destroy the stunned silence as they sound down the street.

"We should get out of here," Ben says, his voice tense.

I nod and he leads us out of the gym to the front doors. Morri scoots out in front of me and darts around the school, her nose to the ground. She seems relatively calm though.

"I didn't drive," I say. My attempt to get him to drive me home seems stupid and pathetic now.

Officers approach us from the parking lot. "What are you kids doing?" one of them asks.

A brief instant of panic passes through me. I hide my crossbow behind me. Luckily I'm behind Ben, so the officers don't notice it.

"Just leaving the dance," Kyle answers with ease. "There was a huge commotion. What's going on?"

The officers exchange significant glances with each other. "There's been calls from the school," another says. "You didn't see anything?"

"We wondered what the mass evacuation was about," Abby says. "We were smoking outside, so we missed it."

I smile at Ben. He nods at me. They had our backs.

"Well, you kids should head on home. We'll check it out."

"Right," Kyle agrees. "We'll just consider ourselves lucky."

We walk away as calmly as we can muster as the officers head inside.

"What now?" Ben asks as the five of us stand in the parking lot.

"Ummm, well, I need a ride."

"I got ya," he says and heads to his truck.

I turn around and look at the school lit up by the lights from the police cars. Another one pulls in.

Grandma was right. I just saw my first freaking werewolf.

CHAPTER 22

Ben

Yup. She's a werewolf slayer. Connolly Clan at that, and I don't think she even knows what that means. If she did, she wouldn't say it so readily. I try to cover my response by keeping my jaw from hitting the floor when she says it, but it isn't easy. She must know the significance of her grandmother's clan. She must know the danger...

My curse is my motivation. I hate what I am. I hate what it does to me. I'm ashamed. What my own mom did to Sam drives me to keep others safe. Some may think it strange, my desire to help destroy werewolves since I am part one, but I'm even more determined to be a hunter, to keep the bad ones contained.

Seems strange, I know, that Sam and I are werewolves. Well, I'm half werewolf. Since Mom, Dad's been obsessed with hunting and tracking them. We don't necessarily kill them unless they've done something terrible or are attacking others, but Dad can track and hunt pretty much any werewolf he sets his mind to. Any one except Mom.

I've never hunted with a girl before, only my Dad and my brothers. They always fight smart and strategic. Becca didn't have the opportunity to be smart and tactical. Her wolfhound dragged her right in the middle of it.

The wolfhound is nowhere to be seen at first, but before I drive away, she appears. Becca ushers her into the bed of the truck. The dog didn't seem to trust me at first. I wonder if she senses something in me. I drive Becca to her grandmother's house, and the others follow.

She digs a key out of her bag and lets us into the house. It's small but well-kept and nice.

"Hi, doggy," I say.

Morrigan sniffs me then takes a step back and runs over to her bed by the fireplace, whimpering. She puts her chin on her paws and watches us.

The others enter and look around. Kyle notices the giant doggy door cut into the kitchen door.

"That door isn't very safe," Kyle says. "Anyone could fit through there."

"The door isn't safe, but Morri is," Becca says. "As are the other dogs on the premises." Behind Becca out the windows, moving dark shapes trot around the yard. "Anyone stupid enough to come through a dog door that big deserves what they get." She drops her purse on the couch. "Come on. I think Mom had a meeting tonight, and Gran is at Bingo at the community center."

"Bingo?" I can't believe one of the most well-known, modern slayers plays Bingo on Friday nights.

"Yeah?" Becca gives me a funny look. She doesn't get who her grandmother is at all.

She leads us upstairs to her room. I'm standing in Becca Redford's room. I'm looking at her bed. She frantically picks up some dirty clothes and throws them in a hamper to tidy up. There isn't a lot of personal stuff in here yet. Some makeup on a vanity table, some clothes and scarves draped on the furniture. A few concert flyers are pinned up. I soak it all in, all of Becca Redford's inner world in.

The room smells like her. It smells like vanilla and lilacs. I'm good at scents. I know these things.

Becca flops down on her bed, legs crossed at the ankles. I head her way, presumptuous, I know, but Maddie sits next to her. Abby pulls out the chair at the vanity table. Kyle grabs the chair at the computer desk. I sit opposite Becca, on the floor. I don't really care. At least I can look at her.

"So? Tell us everything about werewolves and hunters," Maddie says.

"Why don't you start, Ben?" Becca says, looking at me.

I explain the very basics. I tell them they are sworn to secrecy to prevent wide-scale panic, and that if the werewolves were revealed, they'd be more likely to attack. "We keep the secret based on a thousand-year-old pact. They control their ferals if we keep their secret. If we reveal that werewolves do indeed exist, they'll release their ferals to protect their packs and their territories."

Becca keeps her eyes on me. I can tell she's listening intently. I wonder if she knows about any of this or not.

"Ferals meaning the wild werewolves?" Maddie asks.

"Yes, the beasts," I explain. "Some werewolves live in modern society, work normal jobs, control the changing, and abide by the covenant. They don't kill or contaminate innocents; they abide by human laws and laws of God. Others are criminals who don't. They create more werewolves, they kill indiscriminately, and they cause chaos. Those are the ones we hunt, right Becca?"

She tenses, her eyes flashing at me. She seems taken

aback at being called on to respond. "Oh, yeah, right. Those ones."

I feel the need to get rid of the others, so I can press her for what she knows. "Do you want to fill them in on anything?"

"Umm, some of us hunt with hounds, my clan in particular. I think you covered the rest. But yeah, that's it. We kill werewolves, so yeah," she adds.

"We kill *feral* werewolves," I clarify.

"Right, ferals." The word sounds strange coming from her. She says it like she's never uttered it before, like she's testing it out on her tongue.

"So what's the best way to kill a werewolf?" Maddie asks. "Is silver necessary? Does the moon affect anything?"

"Silver doesn't hurt," I tell her. "Wolfhounds are particularly good. I've never seen one in action until today. And as far as the full moon goes, werewolves are affected. It doesn't necessarily force a change, but it hinders control for all werewolves, feral and otherwise. You'll be more likely to catch a werewolf out on a full moon. They suffer from a syndrome on full moon nights. Do you want to explain?" I ask Becca, wondering if she can.

"You're doing fine."

I realize she knows none of this. "They suffer from something called lunacy or FMS." They look at me blankly. "Full moon syndrome."

"Is it like PMS?" Abby smirks.

"A lot like it. It makes a werewolf's hormones go out of whack, and their emotions are heightened. The moon makes the werewolves go a little crazy, even the civilized werewolves who function in society. The moon causes them to act more chaotic than they normally would, like if they were out drinking too much. They will act more emotional and less rational, some more violent and less controlled. Civilized werewolves won't necessarily change into the beast and kill people, but they have to take steps to make sure they are around those they trust, away from large crowds, and can keep to themselves during the twenty-four hours around the full moon. They manage it. They act responsibly during lunacy. Ferals ride through it. They let it take over and enjoy it, like a drug."

Becca

I listen as Ben explains werewolf lore and the pact and hunting to the others. Why didn't I know all this? Why hasn't Grandma told me? Everything I've ever been told centers around the hounds. I was told we kill werewolves. Morri and other wolfhounds sense werewolves. They sense the beasts. Can she sense those walking around in normal society?

"So when the werewolf is in monster form, that means they are ferals," I state this, but it's more of a question to Ben. Will he correct me?

"Most likely. Most civilized werewolves reject their beast form. If they choose to take it, and that's a big *if*, it would be out in the wild somewhere far away from any innocents who may spot them or be injured by them. Civilized werewolves are essentially in deep undercover."

Ben is a werewolf hunter. And he's smart. Maybe we could work together, be a team. He could teach me stuff, and I could teach him about slaying with hounds. God, he's cute, and even cuter when he's explaining stuff.

"How long have you been hunting?" I ask him.

"A little over three years now. Since I turned thirteen. You?"

"Not long. Just since I moved here."

He nods at me and looks down, appearing to be deep in thought. I can tell he knows how little I've been taught.

Morri's footsteps sound on the stairs like a stampede of wildebeests. Dainty isn't her jam, that's for sure. She thunders into the room, stops, and stares at Ben, her ears perking at the curious level. She lowers her head and approaches me slowly, then she head-butts my leg. This is how she hugs me, the top of her head pushing against me.

"Awwww," Maddie says. "She loves you."

I smile as I pet her. She loves me, and I love her. She retreats from the hug then proceeds to sit in front of me, directly between Ben and me. Her eyes don't leave him. She pretty much ignores the others.

I frown, and Ben sits up straight. "I don't think she's seen another werewolf hunter before," I explain.

"Yeah, or she might smell the werewolf blood on me from earlier."

"Right." Or she could be jealous. This is a guy who would actually finally understand me. This guy knows more about my freak show lifestyle than I do. Maybe I could have the homecoming dance with the varsity football player, the dates, the normal life, and all of that after all. And still slay werewolves on the side.

Kyle peers out the window. "I should head home. This is a lot to process. Not to mention, if our parents have heard about the incident at the dance, they'll be worried to death."

Ben stands and brushes his hands on his jeans. "Yeah, right. So please, remember—"

"We won't tell a soul!" Maddie says. She's clearly thrilled to be in on the secret.

Abby crosses her heart with her finger. "Hope to die."

Ben exhales. "Okay, good. Plus, if you did tell, everyone would think you were nuts."

I frown. I'm not sure he needed to sound so harsh.

"Right, okaaaay," Kyle says, flashing Ben an uneasy glance.

The two girls follow him downstairs and head out, too. Ben stays behind after they leave and turns back to me.

"Okay, so what's your *real* story?"

CHAPTER 23

Ben

Thank God the others finally go so I can have a minute alone with Becca. I need to find out what she's doing, if she's for real, what her training is. Here is this beautiful, strong, fearless girl. Here is a girl I could confide in, tell secrets to. This girl out of all the others could understand me. But I don't think she does.

"Excuse me?" she asks.

"What's your real story? It's clear you haven't been taught the werewolf lore or history at all. Has Mrs. Russell taught you anything? Did you know the different types of werewolves?"

She turns away. "No. So? I'm supposed to kill the ones with the teeth and the fangs. That pretty much sums it up, doesn't it?"

She's not completely wrong, but still. "Can you recognize civilized werewolves?"

She turns back to me, then shrugs. "I'm all about the monsters."

I release a breath. "And your training is teaching you how to hunt alone? Just you and your dog?"

She nods.

"That's the saddest thing I think I've ever heard." I lean against the arm of the couch in the living room.

"What? Why?" She crosses her arms in front of her and glares at me.

"I remember my first hunt. I remember my first kill. I had a team to back me up. My older brothers and my dad. Hunting is scary. It's dangerous. What kind of clan sends out a girl alone with a dog to hunt monsters?" We are monsters. I don't know what else to call us. I run my hands through my hair.

"Hey! She's not a dog. She is an Irish wolfhound. She is, in particular, an Irish were-wolfhound bred to kill werewolves, blessed with magic to heighten her abilities."

"She's not immortal, and neither are you."

She turns away from me and stares outside her living room window for several seconds. "The only ones left practicing from the Connolly Clan are my gran and me. All she has is me, so don't blame her if you don't think I'm a star slayer."

And now I feel bad. I detect a crack in her voice. She's still new and has a huge learning curve ahead of her. I hurt her feelings, insulted her and her grandmother. I'm a complete jerk. I hope she doesn't start to cry, or I don't know what I'll do.

I reach out and touch her arm. "Hey, I'm sorry. Come out with me."

She turns halfway around, but she doesn't pull away from my touch. "What do you mean?"

"Next Wednesday night is the full moon. I'm supposed

to patrol the woods. Come out with me. You were going to hunt on a full moon, anyway, right?"

She shrugs.

"Then hunt with me. I'll teach you what I know. Oh, and it's the Fourth of July, so we'll probably see the fireworks, too. It could be fun."

She faces me, and I reluctantly withdraw my hand from her arm. "Yeah?" she asks.

"Yeah. I'll bring snacks." Snacks are good, right?

She laughs. "Okay, and I'll bring the wolfhound."

It's a risk, going out on a full moon. I don't suffer the same effects that full werewolves do, but I have to be careful. I take anti-anxiety medication on full moon nights and I get a mean headache, but I should be able to keep it under control. I need to help her, and she needs actual training. She needs to learn the ropes. And from what I've heard of the Connolly Clan, she needs allies and protection.

Becca

For the next few days, I hardly concentrate on anything else but the impending date. It is a date, right? An evening, a boy and a girl, and food are involved. I think it sounds like a date.

Grandma is away visiting a sick friend, so training has stalled with the exception of what I have planned with Ben. She left early Saturday morning, so I hadn't even told her about my first kill yet.

Things in the neighborhood are weird. On Monday, the school is wrapped up with yellow police tape. According to the paper, the witnesses' stories are jumbled and don't make sense. Since I'm the new girl, no one can identify me as the girl with the crossbow. I wear my hair down the next few days to keep them from recognizing me since I'd worn it up that day.

The police report the incident as an animal attack. I read one report online where Kyle is interviewed. He tells a story about a dogcatcher holding a net and a lead. He poses the theory that the young woman hadn't used a bow, but an extended lead to catch or trap the wild animals. That's why he's the straight-A brainiac, I guess.

I see Ben a few times mowing lawns before our weird hunting date. He only catches me looking at him once. He gives a slight wave. Blood rushes to my face, and I continue on my run.

It doesn't mean anything, I tell myself. He's going to show me hunter stuff, so I don't get killed. It is not a date. It *is* a date. I don't know what it is. God! What should I wear? Each day I lay out a different outfit. Monday I lay out what I figure to be a slayer outfit: black cargo pants, army boots, black tank top, black army jacket. I paint my nails black. I even lay out a black military beret.

Tuesday I decide I'm being ridiculous. I'm not on a SWAT team. I lay out something more date-y. My flower-embroidered jeans, a ruffled tank, and a suede, tan biker jacket. I take off the black polish and paint my nails coral.

Wednesday I try something a bit more date night and more hunter night combined: black tank dress, black riding boots, and a gray leather jacket I steal from Mom's closet. I add a long chain with a big crystal on the end. Okay, it isn't completely slayer mode, but it's cute, and there probably won't be any slaying anyway. Plus, we're supposed to be training. I'm hoping for more hanging out than hunting, but we'll see.

Apparently he got my number from Maddie when he was at the pizza place. He texts me that he'll come by my place after dinner as most of the action won't start until sundown. My filthy mind wonders what he means by that, but I'm a wreck Wednesday. I remove the ugly coral nail polish and change to lavender. Mom gets home from work and makes supper while I fret in my room. I dress and change again a million times, but go back to the tank dress, and that's where I am when Mom calls me down. She's made salmon, asparagus, and homemade bread.

"I'm just having salad," I tell her.

She flops her arms at her sides and exhales. "Fine. I made all of this for the two of us. Your grandmother isn't back from staying with Grace yet."

"When is she supposed to be back?"

"It's hard to say. It depends on her friend."

"I hope everything is okay."

Mom uses the tongs to put some salad on my plate. "When you get to be her and her friends' age, things are less and less okay."

"That is morbid, Mom." I put some salad dressing on and start to eat. I feel bad now that she made this big meal just for me. Cooking isn't her thing, really. But I'm too nervous to eat, plus Ben is bringing snacks. Though I don't want to look like a pig in front of him.

"Okay, I'll have some salmon, too," I say.

She smiles and puts some on my plate.

Finally, she looks at me. She's been in her own little world since we've moved here. She's barely had a conversation with me about something real, about something other than chores and things I might want from the store.

She frowns. "Why are you all dressed up?"

"I have a date! Sort of…" I explain.

"With that Hunt boy?"

I nod and eat. I leave out the werewolf slayer part and leave in the romantic fun part, which may not even exist. I don't think Mom cares as much about the Hunt and Redford family rivalry as Grandma does. If Grandma were here, I might censor that part out.

"Okay, then, home by midnight," she tells me. "Weird things are happening lately. First that girl then the thing at the dance."

Yeah, so I hadn't told her about the dance or me slaying my first werewolf either. Mom tends to avoid talking about all things werewolf slaying. She has been too preoccupied to connect the dots that I was at that dance.

I'm putting my plate in the sink when I hear the knocking on the kitchen door. "Come on, Morri."

Mom gives me an odd look. "Why are you taking the dog?"

I probably shouldn't have left the slaying part out.

CHAPTER 24

Ben

I'm sort of nervous. I know this isn't a date, but still. It could be. I showered and shaved and put on my red Kansas City Chiefs hoodie. My knife rides on my hip, and my brass knuckles are in my pocket. The snacks are in my backpack because snacks are important. I'm always starving on hunt nights and full moon nights.

Though it's a full moon, I make sure to take her somewhere we shouldn't encounter anything, a low traffic area. I also make sure to have some aspirin with me. Full moons give me headaches. And I've taken my meds to help me remain even and under control.

I walk over to her place, wishing I had the car. Nic has it for the night. He had to work, so he gets priority. Since I'm youngest, I rarely get priority. I ring the bell.

She opens the door, and I about die. Becca is full-on smoke show. She's been wearing her hair down since the dance. It hits past her shoulders, blonde streaks, wavy. She has big gray eyes and full lips with a bit of gloss. She's wearing black boots and a black minidress. Her legs are killer, and the dress shows just a hint of cleavage. My heart forgets to beat. Damn. I don't know if these are guy hormones or wolf urges or full moon effects or all of the above. How will I ever focus? What was I thinking, going out on full moon night?

She stands there, and I realize I'm gaping at her and not talking, like a moron. I'm supposed to say something now. Something smart? Something funny? Something... Anything.

"Hey."

"Hey." She waves, and Morri pokes her head out next to her, staring at me.

Right. Hunting. "So, are you ready?" Dumb question. Of course she's ready. She's standing there gorgeous, everything put together, everything perfect. What more would she need to get ready?

"Yeah."

"You look—" Shit, am I supposed to comment on how pretty she is? This is supposed to be a friendly training session. Her looks don't matter. Is that sexist? The first thing out of my mouth is me judging her level of attractiveness. God, I try to shut myself up. "Ready. You look ready. Let's go."

God, she's beautiful. I can't think straight. This is going to be a long night.

Becca

I look ready? Did he just say that? What does that even mean? Guys are so dumb. "So where to?"

He stares at me blankly. What the hell?

"Ben, where are we going?"

"Oh, right, uhhhh…" He looks up and down the street. "The woods."

"Sketchy," I say, teasing.

"No, it's fine. It should be fine. Though it is a full moon. We should be fine."

He's stammering. I'll take credit for that and accept it as a compliment.

I smile at him. "I'm joking."

He laughs. "Right. Let's go."

We head to the woods to cut through to the high school. Morri trails behind. She doesn't need a leash with me. I've been working with her lately. She will follow my commands now.

Ben and I chitchat about our week and what updates we've heard about the werewolf attacks so far as we delve into the woods. It's cute and easy and feels normal. It's so rare that I have a chance to feel normal. I'm laughing at his jokes, and he's smiling. And the best part is that he knows I'm anything but normal, and I know he's anything but normal.

And he's totally hot. He's taller than I remember. His hair is sort of messed on top, and a bit of stubble is scattered along his strong jaw. And those eyes. I gaze into them as he's telling me something stupid another footballer said, and though it's dark out, I realize something.

"You have one blue eye and one brown eye!" I take his chin in my hand and turn his face slightly, so I can double-check myself.

He seems embarrassed. "Oh, that, yeah."

"That's adorable." It just came out. What is wrong with me?

"You think so?" He looks down at me, and our eyes lock for a few seconds.

The sky's darkened, but the moon gives us plenty of illumination, and a slight chill runs up my back. Up my short dress more like. I shiver.

"Here," he says, taking off his sweatshirt and putting it around my shoulders.

"You'll freeze," I protest.

"Nah, I don't get cold. Feel." He puts the back of his warm hand against my cheek.

"Oh, wow," is all I manage. He's really hot-blooded. I imagine taking his hand and kissing it, then pulling it down around to the small of my back and leaning in for a long, real, deep kiss....

"Over here is a good spot. We can watch and have something to eat. I can tell you other hunter stuff."

Hunter stuff. Great. My favorite. I force a smile. "Can't wait." I try to erase all sarcasm from my tone.

Ben

I need an aspirin in a bad way. The moon is beating down on me. It pulls at my blood and sometimes triggers migraines in me. It's ringing in my head. But I haven't had a forced change in six years, and I was just a kid then. I have it under control. I only change when I need to, when I need the strength and the power.

But here I am with this girl, this amazing girl, and she's seeing me, she's listening to me, she's laughing at my dumb jokes. I should never have brought her out on a full moon. I'll have to keep my emotions in check. I can't be struck by the powers of the moon.

She's freezing, but my blood is running so hot right now, I could go shirtless tonight and not notice. I touch her cheek. She doesn't pull away. I want to hold her against me, kiss those full lips. Get it together, Hunt!

I lead her to the area I usually hang out when on patrol. A fallen tree makes for a decent bench to sit on near the fire pit I dug. The trees shelter me from the full effect of the moon. I stack some of the kindling I'd left last time I was here and take out my lighter.

Her wolfhound keeps eyeing me, though. She obviously suspects there is something up with me but isn't sure what. I'm not feral, and that's all she's been taught. I did some research before coming out with Becca and her wolfhound tonight. Wolfhounds only fully sense ferals, which are werewolves in beast form. So there's that. Plus, I'm only half werewolf anyway. And I'm civilized. And Morrigan has seen me kill. I'm not 100 percent sure what the wolfhound is thinking, but I'm pretty sure she's confused enough not to kill me while I'm talking to Becca.

We sit down. She huddles, adorable in my red hoodie, and I empty my backpack. I'd thought about bringing Cheetos, but then realized they wouldn't be good date food if this is a date. We'd have orange everywhere. So I cut up some apple slices, brought baby carrots, pita bread, and hummus. Seems like a more dignified snack than Cheetos anyway. I also brought some Sprite and a few plastic cups.

"M'lady," I say, trying to be goofy as I pour her something to drink. "Some sparkling wine for you."

She laughs and starts eating. And can she ever eat! I like that.

"Are you still cold?" I'm not sure what other warmth I'd have to offer if she were. My body perhaps? Oh God. Now I'm thinking of that.

"I'm good," she says.

"So, hunting..." I start. "In my family, it's a group thing. My dad got into it around the time I was born. I started informal training once I hit double digits, but we don't actually hunt until our teens."

"How many brothers do you have?"

"Two, older. You?"

"None. Just me. My gran is the one with the experience. She told me some hunting tactics and training tactics. She's my trainer but isn't in shape to ever hunt with me. My mom seems to kind of resent the whole thing, I think, so she doesn't talk a whole lot about it."

"That's sad, then, that you have no one to talk to about it all, except your grandmother. It's a bizarre world."

"Yeah." She watches her hands as she twists a blade of grass around and around.

I'm not sure if it's the moon or me, but I want to help her. I want to take her in my arms and feel her against my chest. She must be so alone, bearing the weight of slaying on her own. I've always had my family. They trained me and helped me control the curse. They never resented me or Sam. I'd never betray them, and I'll never be my mom.

She needs to know about her clan. She needs to know

about the curse. I glance at her as she stares into the fire. She shouldn't deal with this alone.

"Well, you can talk to me." I contain myself, keeping my hands folded, my forearms on my knees as I lean forward. But I look at her, right in the eyes, so she knows I mean it. Right in those gorgeous gray eyes. "Whenever you need to."

Becca

Massive swoon overload. Butterflies threaten to take over my entire body. I shiver, not from the cold, but from the nerves of being near him. I want to kiss him, touch him, make him groan, make him want me like I want him. But he sits there, so controlled, so refined.

I need him. I need a friend to talk to, and I don't mean about hunting. I need someone to hang out with, have fun with, talk for hours about nothing with. I never do any of those things with someone. And there's the slayer training. It takes a toll, for sure. He understands that.

And I need him like a girl needs a guy. I need him to think I'm pretty and to have trouble keeping his hands off me. I haven't properly kissed a guy in ages. I want to kiss him so hard that my toes curl and I see stars.

It really is perfect sitting in the woods, under the moon, talking about things, real things. He's close enough that I can feel his body heat, but he might as well be a thousand miles away because I can't just kiss him. What if he's looking for a training buddy? What if he's looking just to help me out? I think he's interested in me, as much as any high school guy is interested in a halfway decent girl, but I don't know. And what would Grandma say? She's forbidden me to be with him.

What if?

What if I just kiss him? Best case scenario, butterfly fireworks exploding. Worst case scenario, I freak him out and lose this, lose whatever it is we are starting—friendship, partnership, a budding romance. And Grandma disowns me. There's that, too.

God! I'm not shy, that's not it. I just don't want to blow it. If it was some random cute football player, then who cares? That's the problem now. I care. I care about what happens after the kiss. I care about losing him. Already. Even though I've only known him a few months. He's so much more than anyone I've ever known. He's actually killed monsters. He has faced his fears and found his strength and stopped evil.

We have got to start talking about something, or I'm going to jump him, and nothing good will come of that.

"So you didn't mention your mom. Where's she with all of this?"

He deflates in front of my eyes. His body slumps slightly, and his gaze goes right to the ground.

"She's been out of the picture for a while. Years, actually."

"Oh, I'm sorry."

"Nah, it's okay. Perfectly reasonable question."

"So she's not a hunter or is she?"

Ben laughs and shakes his head. "No. She's definitely not a hunter."

He doesn't say anything more, and I decide not to pry. Well, I killed the mood at least. Way to go, Becca.

I should make another bomb joke. That'd be hilarious.

"So how often do you go out on patrol?" I ask him.

"We have a schedule. My brothers and I alternate, so typically every third night. On full moons, though, we usually all go out. It was pretty quiet around here until recently. Sometimes, we travel and hunt other places around the Midwest. Something's been happening here lately. Lots of strange energies at the school. There was the explosion, and after that, it seems a lot of cursed wolves are on the loose."

"How exactly does that work?" I ask.

"Well, werewolves are either born with the curse, get infected, are turned with a ritual, or are directly cursed," he tells me.

"Directly cursed?"

"Yes, by an evil entity of some sort. A devil or a demon, but sometimes a dark witch. Yeah, I'm surprised you didn't know."

"Gran hasn't been completely forthcoming on a lot of the werewolf side of things. She sticks to the stabby, killy side." I shrug and rub my hands together for warmth.

He takes my icy hands in his warm ones and holds them. "I'll tell you anything you want to know."

And that does it! I jump his bones.

CHAPTER 25

Ben

She gazes into my eyes for a second before leaning in and kissing me. At first, I start to pull back, but why? Her lips on mine are amazing. She tastes like I imagine roses would. She comes at me hungry, pulls her hands out of mine, and brings one up behind my head like she doesn't want me to leave. Her kiss is soft but determined, and she opens her mouth slightly. I inhale her vanilla and lilac scent.

As though perfectly cued, I hear the pops and explosions of the Fourth of July fireworks in the background. She kind of laughs while we're kissing, but I don't pull away to look. The better fireworks are right here.

God! God! God! I want her so bad. I let her in and kiss her back, my tongue venturing into her territory. My hands are around her, on her back, pulling her close. She doesn't resist. I kiss her again, and again, wanting her, wanting more, wanting it all. My beautiful girl, my beautiful werewolf slayer, this beautiful creature in front of me. I want to keep kissing her. I want to slide my hands up under her dress. I want to climb on top of her and....

Damn, this moon is making me crazy. She's making me crazy. I want her with every cell in my cursed body, but not like this. I don't want to ruin this because I finally have someone I can talk to about whatever.

But God damn it, she's so receptive. She doesn't retreat, she doesn't pull away at my touch, she grinds in, wants more. I want more. Holy God, help me. The fireworks continue to blast in the skies around us while we remain focused on each other. There is nothing else.

A low growl comes from her were-wolfhound. I fear she must sense my curse. I pull away from Becca and turn to her hound, but Morrigan's not facing me. She stands and her growl bursts into a fierce bark.

Becca pushes me off and grabs for her crossbow.

I'm out of it, suffering from post make-out brain. I want to kiss her again, touch her again. I'm losing it, and the moon and the resulting migraine starts to ring.

"Easy, doggy." A male voice sounds from the darkness of the trees.

Morrigan doesn't ease up.

"Call off the dog," he says.

"Mr. LaRette?" I leap to my feet, hands balled into fists.

I was supposed to be tracking him. I was supposed to be on surveillance. I didn't think one night off would be a big deal.

A growl rolls through Becca's wolfhound again. But LaRette's in human form. A few branches crack behind him, and two werewolf forms flank his sides.

"What the hell?" Becca asks.

I mean really, what the hell? I thought this was supposed to be safe. I didn't think we'd see werewolves. These are only the third and fourth ones I've ever seen. I didn't believe Grandma for so long. I guess all she had to do was take me in the woods. Cuz some guy is hanging out here with werewolves the night of a full moon. That can't be good.

"Stay back," Ben says and steps in front of me.

Morri's growl erupts into frenzied barking. I grab her collar. Should I just let her loose? It's all I can do to keep her down. She leaps and pulls from me. I could quiet her with a word, but I'm okay with her like this at the moment.

"Ben and the new slayer," the man says.

"You're supposed to remain unchanged," Ben says, his body tense and leaning forward.

The strange man looks around, raising his arms to the sides. "But I am."

The two werewolves snarl beside him.

My instinct tells me it's ass-kicking time. Morri is echoing my sentiments, but Ben is holding back. Why?

"And at the dance the other day? What was that?" Ben presses.

"That wasn't me. I'm as surprised as you are," the man says.

"Ben, it's not in my nature or my wolfhound's to stand by while werewolves live and breathe," I tell him.

"Call off your wolves," he says to the man.

The man gives a quick jerk of his head, and the werewolves dash off into the woods. Morri is about to yank my arm off, but I hold on while she snaps and growls after them. She settles slightly when they are out of sight.

"Why are you here?" Ben asks.

"I knew I'd find you here. I wanted to talk about the attack at the school."

Ben scoffs.

"Listen, I'm shocked to find the covenant broken. I'd never act so rashly in my own territory. Other places"—he glances around the woods—"perhaps. But it is in my best interest, as well as yours, to find out where those other wolves came from."

Ben seems to consider this.

Morri still pulls against my grip on her collar.

"Keep the covenant," Ben orders.

"I'll keep mine. You keep yours. You and your Little Red Riding Hood." He points to me.

I realize I'm wearing Ben's red Chiefs hoodie, holding a big bad wolfhound at bay while sitting by a basket of apples and snacks. Weird.

"You deal with yours, and all will be well." He holds up his hands and backs a few steps into the woods, his eyes on Morri, before turning and heading in the direction of the school.

The Fourth of July fireworks sputter away and are over.

I release Morri, who hurries off into the woods sniffing for the werewolves. I give a sharp whistle, and she remains within sight.

"What the hell was that all about?" I ask.

Ben takes a deep breath. "That's Lee LaRette. Remember the guy you punched at Lake Pizza? It's his dad. On paper, he is a civilized werewolf. He appears to keep the covenant. He appears to follow the laws, but we know he's essentially a werewolf mob leader. He's sometimes seen with ferals but claims he can control them. That display just now, it isn't against the agreement, but he teeters on the edge, pushes his limits."

"He can't be trusted."

"Not even a little. We keep close tabs on him, as does your grandmother. We're waiting for him to cross the line, and then we could take him out, but he's clever. We haven't caught him out on anything. None of the ferals want to cross him. He has too many friends protecting him. He has a good reputation in the civilized world. For him to break the pact—"

"It would have to mean something big."

Ben looks at me. "Very."

I ease back down onto the log, and Morri trots back over.

"I'm not terribly excited that he knows about you…and Morrigan." Ben gestures toward her. He shakes his head and runs a hand through his hair. "You're in danger now. Even more than before. The Tony Soprano of the local werewolf pack knows you exist. You and your grandmother are in danger, Becca. I have to protect you. If we don't keep you safe, the werewolves will rise to power, and that will be the end of life as we know it."

CHAPTER 26

Ben

I just said I...I had to protect her. She looks at me with her big eyes, and the moon hammers down on me. My knees go weak. This isn't good. This isn't good at all. Mr. LaRette is bad news. Becca knows so little about our world, so little about her own clan, so little about me.

But I know about it. I can teach her. I can help her.

I have to help her. She doesn't even know about the Connolly curse. What will she do when she finds out about me?

"I don't need protecting. I could have taken all three of them out with Morri." Her jaw is set, and she stands with a hand on her hip.

I believe her.

"I know you could have, and you would've broken your hand again." I look at her and want to kiss her again, hold her again. I change strategies. She doesn't even know what she's up against.

"Becca, I'm going to tell you something. Maybe you

already know, and maybe you don't, but you need to." I take a deep breath. "You and your grandmother are the last of the Connolly Clan. My dad has been studying this werewolf stuff for years now. What that means, what he's learned is that when the Connolly Clan falls, the others start to as well. The training, the lore, all of it fades away. The end of the first clan of werewolf slayers signals the end of all of us." I give her a pointed look.

"The first clan?" she asks, and I realize she knows less about it all than I thought.

"When you and your grandmother are gone, all of the clans will die off. We already are. Slayers and hunters are a rare breed. But once you and especially your grandmother are gone...first the few remaining clans that use wolfhounds, then the hunters, one by one, will all die off, and the werewolves will claim the world as theirs. That's why you need to be protected. Your family started this werewolf fighting back in Ireland hundreds of years ago." I step toward her, and she doesn't step away. She's unafraid. She holds her ground. I take the uninjured hand that is stubbornly planted on her hip and hold it with both of mine. "Not because I think you can't protect yourself, but because you are all of the clans. The longer you survive, the longer all slayers and hunters do." I can't help myself. I take her hand to my mouth and kiss it.

She looks at me, full of questions.

"Will you let me help you?" I ask her.

She nods though questions still dance in her eyes. "Teach me what else I need to know."

He makes me crazy. I lean in and kiss him and never want to stop. I don't know why. I don't know if it's his different colored eyes or his strong shoulders. I don't know if it's because he's so smart and skilled and knows about stuff that I should know more about. I don't know if it's the way he looks at me like he wants to devour me and save me at the same time. I don't know, but I want him and want to be close to him. Unfortunately, the kiss ends.

"You'll let me help you?" he asks, and the way he asks it holding my hand, I half expect him to take a knee and declare his loyalty to me forever. My sworn knight.

I nod.

"Let me take you home. We'll start tomorrow. Every day if you can."

I nod again. "Yeah."

"We should talk to your grandmother, too. And whatever you do, don't tell anyone else you're a slayer or that you're from the Connolly Clan. It makes you a target. Promise?"

I nod vigorously. "Okay, yeah." He's still holding my hand. It's making me kind of crazy.

"At least you have a different last name. Okay, let's get you home." He kicks dirt over his small fire and gathers up the basket of food.

I'm bummed to be leaving. We were just getting to the good part. We walk home and stay rather quiet.

"I had a good time, I mean before that LaRette guy..." I say as we near my house.

He smiles. "Yeah, before that ass showed up, I was having a really good time."

"Yeah." I smile and feel the blood rush to my face.

"Tomorrow. Can I come over?" He walks me up the back steps to the kitchen door. Morri trots up behind us.

"Yeah, sounds good." I try to sound casual. I open the front door, and Morri lumbers in.

"You're okay with me helping you?" he asks. "I could have my brothers or my dad—"

"I want you," I say, kind of realizing how that sounds when I say it, but sometimes I go for shock value. Sometimes I just say what I want and save time.

He stops and looks at me, his eyebrows raised at first. Then his eyes narrow in on me. He looks at me for a long time, the full moon peeking over his shoulder in the distance. Stray fireworks pop around the lake, holdouts who waited for the community fireworks show to end, shooting them off their docks.

"I want you, too. God, so much." He reaches up and brushes my hair behind my ear. Warmth radiates from his thumb as it grazes my cheek. He leans in and kisses me.

I gasp. Everything explodes inside me, and the world goes numb. The kiss doesn't last nearly long enough.

"I will help you through this," he says.

I swoon almost to death.

"I think you will," I tell him. "Oh, your hoodie." I realize I'm still wearing it and start to take it off.

"Keep it. It suits you, Red."

I smile like a dumbass.

"See you tomorrow," he says, backing down the stairs.

"Can't wait." I close the door behind me and lean on it.

I know part of slaying is all about work, but part of it is about Ben, and me, and making out on a full moon night, and maybe even a school dance or two. We can do this whole high school romance thing, and we can kick some major bad guy werewolf ass while we do it.

CHAPTER 27

I'm happy to see Grandma is back, especially because she's making my ultimate favorite breakfast of biscuits and gravy.

I stumble into the kitchen half awake, stretching. "When'd you get back?"

"This morning. Want some?" She offers me a biscuit.

"Yes!" I grab a knife and cut it in two.

She spoons some sausage gravy over it. She always puts lots of pepper in it. I love it.

"How's your friend?"

She sighs. "She's hanging in there. It's hard when you get to be my age." She stirs the gravy on the stove, facing away from me.

I don't know how to respond to that, so I eat. Morri thunks down at my feet, her usual position.

"So, Gran, what's this about the Connolly Clan and the last of the slayers?" I just blurt it out. I have no time for tact, and really she should've told me already.

Her shoulders slump, and she stops with the spatula in the skillet for a minute. "It's just a theory, Becca."

"One I should be aware of."

"Just a theory, but we are the last of the slayers who use wolfhounds. Ours are the last of the Culain line. When ours die off, it will be a different world, but I wouldn't be taking much stock in fables about us dying and werewolves overtaking the world." She still stares at the stove instead of me.

"Why not?"

"Because there's good in this world. Good that won't let the bad guys win. There always has been. There always will be. People care about each other, and people care about the world around them. Someone will step up. I'm not going to be so vain as to think that our family is holding the world together all on its own." She turns to me.

Fair enough, I guess.

"We can't worry about what other people do or plan. We can only control what we do. Simple as that." She shrugs.

She seems less determined than she usually does. Her eyes are lined and her face and body relaxed or tired or exhausted. Her gaze wanders to Morri under the table, then away.

"You're worried about your friend?"

She gives a little laugh. "I worry about a lot of things, but it does no good to worry about things I can't control. I will help her as best as I can. That's all I can do."

I eat some more and sneak Morri a piece of biscuit.

"How's your hand?" she asks me.

"Better. A little sore but no biggie." I grab a glass and pour some orange juice. "I've been thinking.

"That's never good."

"Thanks, Gran. No, about this spell to cure werewolves. I had a run-in with Mr. LaRette—"

She jerks around to face me. "Becca!"

"It wasn't a big deal. We were in the woods—"

"Becca Belle Redford!"

Crap, she used my full name.

"Who is *we* exactly?" Her eyes narrow. Her arms are crossed, and she holds that spatula menacingly towards me.

Crap, why do I ever open my big mouth.

"No one. Ben. It doesn't matter!"

She shakes her head and turns back to the stove, which has been turned off for several minutes. "It matters."

"Gran, anyway. Listen. LaRette came to talk to us about the werewolves at school. The attack at the dance? I was there. I killed my first werewolf... Well, Morri did. Ben killed the other one. He helped me, Gran. Again."

She turns slowly to me. "So you saw them then?"

"Yes, I saw two more with LaRette in the woods. That's what I'm telling you."

"Morrigan took one out? We owe her a big fat steak. Why didn't you tell me?"

I don't know why I didn't. My head is full of so many things. Full of Ben.

"Were you hurt?" she asks.

"No. Almost. I missed my shots. Ben took the monster out just as it was about to destroy me."

She points her spatula at me. "Work on that crossbow, girl."

"Gran! LaRette says there are other werewolves behind the attacks.

"Of course he says that. What do you expect him to say?"

"Gran, I just think we could work out that spell. You said you knew a witch—"

"I don't know, Becca."

"I need to do something. I can't just sit here. You wanted me to be a slayer. You wanted me to take over. You've trained me. Now let me slay or get rid of werewolves however I can!"

She turns to me. "Okay, I'll see what I can do. You, however, need to work with that crossbow and with Morrigan." She glances at my wolfhound.

"She was amazing the other night," I tell her.

"You need to bond. I see you work well together, but...."

"But what?"

She looks at me and takes a deep breath. "Come here."

I follow Grandma outside, and Morri follows me. Grandma walks to the center of the yard and gives a sharp whistle. All of the dogs on the property trot up to her. Even the puppies come bounding after their mother from the barn. I smile. It's super cute. She pets on them and loves them.

After they've all been loved on and cooed to, Lugh, her oldest Irish wolfhound, limps out of the barn and comes to her. His tail wags slowly, his head down, almost as though he were shy. She turns to him, and the other dogs fall away. He reaches her and puts the top of his head against her leg, his tail wagging lazily, but probably as fast as it can.

She pets him. "Who's a good boy?" she says to him in baby talk. "My best boy. My Lugh bear."

It's terribly sweet. He licks at her hand, and she gazes back at him.

"Did you know," she begins, her voice cracking slightly, "that wolfhounds are one of the few breeds to look you in the eye? They make eye contact and hold it. They're very intuitive and read emotions really well."

At her display of emotion, Lugh becomes more forceful with his head loves, pushing on her leg and pawing toward her, as if he's desperately trying to comfort her.

She squats down next to him and kisses his face, petting and loving on him. It's adorable, really.

"Some slayers use their hounds as weapons. Some call them JAFDs."

"What?"

"JAFD. Just An F'ing Dog. And those people are okay slayers. But these dogs aren't just f'ing dogs. These dogs have empathy, and when you bond with them, it's even more. Lugh here can sense when I'm in trouble or hurt or happy. And when you bond with them, you can sense their feelings, too."

"Well, how do I bond with Morri?" I certainly don't feel what she's feeling, though I did sense that she was near the night of the dance.

She sighs and shakes her head. "You just do, or you don't. You have to spend time with her, work with her. It'll happen. But it's a blessing and a curse." She goes back to loving on Lugh. "When something happens to him...."

She trails off, but I don't need her to finish that sentence.

Ben

I work with Becca most days the rest of the summer. It's amazing. I don't want to do anything else. We train by running, practicing her crossbow, sparring, swimming, kayaking. She brings Morrigan, who is always watching me, waiting. I dread the start of school. I never want the summer to end.

School starts fresh on the heels of another missing girl. Another girl, younger than Kate found in the woods. My dad and brothers and I have scoured those woods, but haven't found any werewolf lairs or hideouts. Sam even shifted to wolf form to get a better sense of the area, but nothing came up. I even considered bringing Becca and Morrigan with us, but Dad didn't think it would be a good idea.

School starts and I hope it doesn't change things with Becca and me. I hope she doesn't ditch me for other friends. Maddie, Abby, and Kyle hang out with her a lot and invite me to lunch. I pull away from my football friends to hang at Becca's table more often. Seems to make sense. Her table knows my secret. Well, they know the outer limits of my secret. They don't know about me yet.

I decided not to change classes to meet Becca's schedule. I thought that might be a little weird, especially since she'd already seen my schedule. I did get moved into drama with her though. Our first class together.

She waves me over next to her, and the new teacher comes into the class. Ms. Eden had to replace Ms. McNair who blew up the school last year. Ms. Eden comes in looking like Morticia Addams, long dark hair, big dark eyes, a deep burgundy dress with drapey sleeves. Drama teacher. Figures she'd be dramatic. She speaks in a British accent, her voice kind of hypnotic. Becca and I give each other a look and try not to laugh.

Becca

My first class with Ben is interesting to say the least. Our teacher is a major hippy goth woman. Must've lived through the 70s, though she doesn't seem very old at all. She's the drama teacher, so it's probably all an act.

The rest of my classes are pretty bland, but I think that of most of school. I have a few classes with Maddie and Abby. One with Kyle, though he's mostly in advanced classes. My focus isn't really on school. It's on finding out where this werewolf nest is.

My moonstone necklace has remained cold, so it's no help. Morri is with me a lot less now that I'm in school, but I do walk through the woods on the way, and she hangs out behind the tree line. I guess it's her way to be on patrol. She's not a normal dog, so we aren't afraid she'll go terrorizing the neighborhood. Grandma says she'll stay in the woods unless there's trouble, and then she'll snap to. No one else needs to worry about her.

I feel safe with her there.

After the first week of school is over and I'm in a groove, Grandma announces, "I've heard of someone who could help with the spell."

"The spell?" Stupid me, I've already lost my slayer mindset.

"The cure spell. It's a ritual, so quite complex. I can't cast it. I say we forget it and just kill them all," she tells me. She's still got a thing against helping or curing werewolves.

"Who can do it or teach it?" I ask.

"I was told they will find us."

"Told by who?"

Grandma shrugs. "Whom, girl. Learn grammar."

Eye roll. "Cuz grammar will kill werewolves."

She ignores me. "I don't really know. There is an underground slayer network I use. Everything is anonymous. You put in a request, and someone gets back to you. I put in a request, though I don't like to. The whole things seems a little sketchy to me, but I knew you'd want me to."

"Okay, thanks. So we just wait?"

She nods. "It's a dark moon, so we should be okay."

"What does that mean?" I blurt out before remembering it was in one of those damn books I read and already forgot.

She looks over her glasses at me. "Becca Belle! It means that werewolves won't be out in the light, in the open, so people should be safe. But it also means they're in the dark, hiding, scheming. Neither are good, but on dark moons, werewolves are less likely to hunt."

"All righty then," I say.

And then we wait.

CHAPTER 28

Becca

I told Ben over the weekend about the weird supernatural network Grandma mentioned. He had no idea what I was talking about.

I gather my books and stand to leave drama when Ms. Eden stops me. "Becca, may I speak with you?"

I give Ben a confused look and shrug. He and the rest of the class leave without me. No other students file in, so this must be Ms. Eden's off-hour.

I go to her desk, and she ruffles through some papers. She eventually finds what she is looking for and hands a paper to me.

"What is it?"

"It is the spell you were looking for." She says it so matter-of-factly, I frown.

"Huh?"

She nods her head at the paper. "The cure spell. It is complex. It will probably take a while to cast. And it requires two very important ingredients that you may not be able to find."

She says all of this without the use of contractions, which is typical for her, and her voice, though soft, is serious and to the point. I skim the page and see a lot of words in a language I don't understand.

"I can't read this."

"No, you probably cannot."

"How can I cast it?"

"You could try to learn Aramaic by the next full moon, or spend a longer time to learn it."

"Learning things isn't my strong suit," I tell her.

She giggles. "I know."

I frown. Geez, I've only had her a week. "So what do I do with this?"

"You should get someone to cast it for you."

"Like who?"

"I guess like me."

"Would you cast it for us?"

"I would," she says. She isn't much for conversation. She just answers the question posed, leaving me wanting to know a lot more information.

"Okay, when?"

"First you need to know whom to cast it upon. Then you would need to know where they are going to be. Then you will need a time, preferably a full moon obviously." She says the last word with zero tone or attitude.

"Okay," I say. I'm thinking this is a lot of stuff, and we haven't even gotten to the spell yet. "Is that all?"

"No."

I slump and lift up my hands. "What else?"

"The two ingredients I mentioned."

I scan the paper again to see if there's an ingredients section. I still can't read Aramaic.

"And they would be…"

"Blood from a werewolf and a sister of the moon."

"I'm sorry, I need what now?"

"Other bodily fluids could work as well, but are not as easy to gather. You need to join the two drops together on the night of a full moon, within range of those you want to cure. The ritual can take several minutes, so the subjects would need to remain in the area until it is complete."

Well, this just got a whole lot more fucking crazy.

Ben

Becca is pale as she exits the classroom. I'm late for my next class, but I don't care. I should find out what that was about.

"She gave me the spell." She shows it to me, and it looks like mumbo jumbo.

"She did?"

Becca nods. "Remember, her identity is a secret, like ours."

"Okay, I know." I'm not the outing type. "Well that's great, isn't it?"

"It's not that simple. We need to know where the werewolves are, when they'll be there, keep them there, get Ms. Eden to cast this spell. Oh! And I need werewolf blood and sister of the moon blood. How am I supposed to get that?

I know the answer. I don't know how to tell her. "Umm, I can ask my dad," I offer.

"Oh!" She lights up. "What happened to the bodies of the werewolves we killed at the dance? Maybe if we could get some blood from them, we could join it with mine."

"It's probably dried up by now, and I don't know what they did with them. If they were smart, they burned them. That was weeks ago. I'm sure they aren't still at the coroner's office anymore."

She deflates. "It all seems so hopeless."

I hate seeing her like this. She doesn't know how easy the werewolf blood piece is. I have it. "Let's focus on finding the werewolves first."

"Good idea. Not that that's much easier." She shoves the spell in her binder.

"True. The sheriff and my dad are already looking for the killer. I don't really know what else to do."

"That's easy," Kyle says from behind me.

I hadn't even heard him and the others walk up. I turn to see him, Abby, and Maddie.

I frown. "How so?"

"How do you trap wolves? We just need to set some bait."

Abby and Maddie nod behind him.

"Set some bait?" I ask.

"Yeah, it's not rocket science, though if it were, I'd probably understand it somewhat better," he goes on. "My uncles hunt deer and things. They made me go out with them my whole life to make me a man or some macho bullshit. Apparently, they don't think being intelligent is masculine. I don't get it."

Maddie nudges him. "Go on."

"So yeah, we were talking"—he points to Maddie and Abby—"and think if we can help you find the werewolves, then you can kill them or whatever you do."

Becca leans in. "Okay."

Kyle unrolls a piece of paper against the lockers and shows us a map of the area. "So we were looking here. The first attack was in the national forest here." He shows us the X he's used to mark it. "The second was here at the school, and the third was over here. I mean if you use triangulation..." He draws lines to the three of them. "The best bet for an encounter would be somewhere in here. It's not 100 percent, but this area is clearly their hunting grounds." He taps the center of the triangle, right in the heart of the Mark Twain National Forest.

The corners of Becca's mouth draw down and she nods. "Interesting theory."

"My brothers and I have patrolled that area pretty thoroughly," I argue.

"You aren't the target, sporto," Abby pipes up.

"Huh?"

She points at the Xs on the map. "Teen girl, school dance, teen girl." She chews her gum and raises her eyebrows at me.

"Okay, so..."

"So the werewolves or whoever are going for single, young girls, with the exception of the school dance. I'm not sure what that was about. Do you think they'd attack a group of guys who are probably loaded up with weapons? Or do you think they'd attack an innocent young girl, alone...in the dark...in the woods?" She nods toward Becca and Maddie.

"You're suggesting one of you go out alone in the woods to draw them out?"

"I'm suggesting we make it look like one of us is alone in the woods to draw them out," Abby says.

"Then the rest of us or your brothers or your dog or whoever are there can jump them!" Maddie says, thrilled to spoil the end for us.

"It's dangerous." I dismiss it outright.

Becca cocks her head. "But it makes sense."

"You can't be serious!"

"Do you have a better idea?" she asks me.

I sigh and wish I were a better idea guy.

CHAPTER 29

Becca

It's a good idea, I have to admit. Not only that, it's the only idea on the table. We plan a few baiting attempts, starting with Maddie, then Abby, and then me closer to the full moon.

Ben helps prepare us for them. He explains how werewolves are scent motivated and tells us to smell as female as possible.

"I'm sorry, what?"

"Well, I mean if they're going after girls, we want you to be like girls," he says.

Abby narrows her eyes at him. "We are girls, idiot."

"No, I mean…" He sighs heavily and runs his hands through his hair. "Okay, my dad found out a few things about the victims."

We stare at him until he finishes his thought. He gives me a look like he wants me to rescue him.

"Well, the girls all smelled…girly…." He churns his hand like he wants us to finish the sentence.

"Girly like flowers?" I ask.

He shakes his head.

"Are we playing charades with this, for real?" Abby snaps.

"Fruity like strawberries?" I ask again. What the hell does girly smell like?

"No." He's blushing now. He takes a deep breath.

Kyle is watching him intently, his hand on his chin.

"Like only girls can smell like!" Ben blurts out.

I'm still frowning, confused. Kyle's eyes widen, and he nods slowly. I glance to the other girls to see if they know what only girls can smell like.

"They were on their periods," Abby says.

"Yes! Thank you."

"Gross," Kyle says.

"It's not gross," Maddie argues. "It's natural."

"Yeah, dumbass," Abby adds.

Kyle holds his hands up and surrenders.

"God, you guys, how hard is it to say that? You think you'd start yours by saying the word?" Abby shakes her head.

"Okay, so I'm confused. We can't just smell girly on command," I say.

"Look at your calendars, ladies. Sync up," Kyle advises.

Abby glares at him. "How do you propose we do that, genius?"

"Don't ask me. I just mean maybe we can schedule patrols at those times that only you can sort out."

The other two look at each other and nod. Oh great, so now I have to share personal stuff. Maddie and Abby start counting and jotting things down, then look at me, their brows raised.

"Don't look at me!" I tell them. "I'll just go on the full moon."

"Is that when you start?" Maddie asks.

"Well, no."

"Well, when?"

"Well, never," I tell her, my voice low, but the guys can still hear.

"What, you never…"

"I did, but I don't anymore because…the pill."

Maddie and Abby don't seem fazed, but Kyle's jaw drops, and Ben turns white.

Great. Now they think I'm a slut.

Ben

Holy shit. I don't even know what to think about that. I'm torn. I'm both excited and concerned at the same time. On the pill? What? Why? And what business is that of mine? And how does that even matter to me? And why do I care? And my mind is going a mile a second. And again, I know I should say something because it's been quiet too damn long, but my words would spill out like alphabet soup if I tried to speak coherently right now.

"Cool," Abby says.

"It's not a sex thing!" Becca says. "It's a medical thing!"

"You don't have to explain." Maddie puts her hand on Becca's arm. "Even if it was sex, who cares? We're in high school. High schoolers have sex. Big deal. Good for you for being prepared."

"Well, it's not a sex thing," she says again.

"It doesn't matter." Kyle has composed himself, and he gives me a nudge with his glance. "Does it?"

I have to say something. I have to say something. I have to say something. He threw me a softball. I have to say something. "No, of course not!"

Becca's shoulders relax. "Okay, then. I mean, I guess I could carry something on me, like raw steaks or something to attract them. Would that work?"

"It couldn't hurt," Kyle says. "And then after, we could BBQ!"

"It's fine," I say. "It's just a theory the coroner's office had and shared with Dad. It could be nothing. But, anyway, they'll also smell your dog, so Morri will have to be downwind, or perfumed to mask her scent. And oddly enough, both victims also had food on them in backpacks."

"Seriously?" Abby asks. "Like these are actual dogs or something. Freaks."

I try not to take offense, but I'm part werewolf, so I know how important scent is. Food, blood, predators, prey. I also realize other than the vanilla lilac scent I catch off Becca's skin, that's always been the only thing I've gotten from her. It's stronger when she's just out of the shower. I can smell the water and the soap still on her skin when that's just happened. And there goes my thought process....

"Are you okay?" she asks me.

"Oh, yeah, ummmm, I was just thinking about how good that is for you."

"What's that?"

"They won't smell you coming," I say.

Everyone stares at me blankly.

"That's good...I guess." She looks at me like I'm a weirdo.

"Yeah, it is."

We plant our bait a few nights later, Maddie on the trail in the woods, walking along with a backpack of snacks. We wait around the same time of night the others were thought to be killed, the rest of us concealed in the bushes. Nothing happens.

Four nights later, it's Abby's turn. Same routine as before. Nothing happens.

Five nights after that, it's Becca's turn. Morrigan's back in the tree line, not with anyone in particular, but Becca tells her to stay, so she stays. Nothing eventful happens in the woods, so we start to head home.

"Well, it was an idea," Kyle says.

"It was a good one, too," Abby tells him. "We could try again."

"The full moon is tomorrow," Becca says. "We have no idea where they are or where they will be."

"And homecoming is tomorrow," Maddie says, bouncing on the balls of her feet.

"Already?" Kyle asks. "I never pay attention to those things."

"Yes, it's early this year. It's tomorrow," Maddie says and gives me a pointed look for some reason.

Becca flushes red. I can see it in the moonlight even. Oh, was that for my benefit? I should ask her. I haven't even been thinking. Shit.

"We have more important things to deal with than homecoming, Maddie," Becca says. "But we shouldn't do anymore bait plants until after the full moon. It will be too dangerous now. Tonight, I was sure...."

Barking sounds in the distance. Morri stops and lifts her head, her ears forward.

We get to the edge of the woods where Abby parked.

"Want a ride?" she asks. Maddie and Kyle take her up on it.

"I'll walk with Becca," I say.

Becca snuggles into my Chiefs hoodie that she wears a lot, I've noticed. A cool wind is starting to blow.

"Okay. See ya," Abby says, with no subtext.

"Byyyyyeeee, you two," Maddie says, also with no subtext. It's all main text.

Becca rolls her eyes and shakes her head. "Sorry about her."

"Why?" I shouldn't make her say it, but I want her to say it. I want to put it all on the table.

"She's just, I don't know. Wants to play matchmaker."

"Is that so bad?" I ask.

She smiles but continues facing forward, Morri trotting at her side. "I don't know. Is it?"

Nice. Deflects it back to me. I take her arm. "Do you want to go to the dance with me?" Yes, I did it right this time.

She looks at me with her big eyes and smiles. "Yeah, I kinda do."

"Yeah? Kinda? Well, I don't think I'll get a better answer than that. Good. I'd like that."

"Would you?"

"I would." I lean in and give her a little kiss. "You know, I meant to ask you to that summer dance, too, but I screwed that all up."

"You did, didn't you?"

I laugh. "Totally." I take her hand and hold it as we walk down the road to her grandmother's house.

A low growl ripples through Morrigan.

Becca instantly freezes. "What is it, girl?"

In the distance, the barking sounds more frantic now,

and wailing, coming from Becca's. I doubt that Becca can, but I get a whiff of smoke on the air.

"Gran!" Becca says as more of a gasp than a word.

Morrigan is off like a shot. Becca drops my hand and is quickly on her heels.

CHAPTER 30

Becca

I beat it to Grandma's as fast as possible, thankful for the first time for all of the running she had me do this summer. Luckily I still have my crossbow slung across my back in case we saw any werewolves on our bait attempt. Morri is way ahead of me, her ears flying. She doesn't pause to bark; she just tears down the road as fast as she can.

The wolfhounds never freak out like this. I've never heard them all in an uproar. Not when the mail carrier delivers a package. Not when a cat strays into the yard. Not when I roughhouse with Morri for fun. Never. So hearing this loud chorus scares the shit out of me. Not only that, but the emotion in the barking is intense. I can almost feel it. The barks are angry and intimidating, but some sound hurt or scared, too. I don't want them hurt. I don't want Gran hurt!

Then comes something even more terrifying than the loud barking. The quieting of it. First one goes silent, then another, until only a few are barking. Then nothing.

I have no idea what happened to Ben or the rest of the world.

An orange glow comes from our property ahead, followed quickly by the scent of smoke. There's a fire. The closer I get shows me the source. The barn.

My mind goes strategic. The hose is on the spigot on the back of the house. I mentally make my plan to get to the hose first, aim it on the fire, call the fire department, find Mom, Grandma and the wolfhounds. Oh God. The wolfhounds are usually in the barn, but they can leave. There's the doggy door on the barn. I'm sure they got out. Why couldn't they get out?

There aren't any lights in the house or anyone coming to help yet. I turn on the spigot and start unfurling the hose. Morri leaps through the dog door into the house. Checking on anyone there? But the house isn't on fire.

"Gran?" I shout as I pull the hose as close to the barn as possible and aim the water toward the fire. Then I hear whimpering coming from inside. What the fuck? I whistle in case the wolfhounds are too disoriented to come out the doggy door to safety. "Come on, wolfhounds!" I call, but they don't come.

Smoke is starting to billow out the window, and orange flames lap at the windows farther back in the barn. A board has been placed at an angle against the doggy door, bracing it closed. The dogs are trapped. Not only that, but someone intentionally trapped them!

"Shit!" I say, dropping the hose and dashing toward the doggy door to free them.

Before I get to where the heat is too much to keep me back, I feel a sharp blow to the side of my head. I hit the ground, and everything goes dark.

Ben

Damn, she and her wolfhound are fast.

I take out my phone and call my brother first. All I say when Nic answers is, "Fire at Mrs. Russell's. Need help." I turn it off and run as fast as I can to the house.

I can't keep up with them in human form, so I think about whether to shift of not. How critical will the minute or so that I could save by shifting be? Is it worth it?

Every shift brings me closer to becoming a werewolf—heart, mind, and soul. Every shift lures us to remain in wolf form. It's tempting. It's addictive. I try not to do it. I try to keep my humanity. Now, though, I can help by doing so. Do I risk going one step closer? How many shifts do I have in me before I lose control and give in to the pull of the moon?

The fire blazes in front of me, and Becca whistles and shouts. Her voice is frantic. I shift. No more thinking. No more debating. I shift to save her, to help her, to protect her.

I embrace the wind. I stop the clouds in front of the moon. I reach inward to my primal self and allow the change to come. Before I realize it, I'm running on all four legs. Faster than my human form. Picking up more scents than I had before. Seeing things and hearing things that weren't completely clear a minute ago.

Run. Use my senses. Breathe. Watch. Listen. Growl. Feel the air.

I smell smoke and flame. Fire in the barn.

Werewolf blood. Four in the house. Becca is in danger. She will be watching the fire.

I leap into the air and crash through the front windows of the living room, landing on another werewolf inside. Human in form but werewolf blood runs through him. I can smell it. My teeth clamp down on his throat. I tear and taste the blood. Clamp down, bite, tear, claw. Use everything sharp to push and rip and cause as much damage as possible. A growl rolls through me as I look up from the one I've defeated, limp beneath me. Four werewolves in human form are left. I smell someone familiar. It makes no sense.

"Ben, that's enough," one says to me.

My human self knows the voice. My human self tries to pull me back in. My human self tries to order me to stand down. My human self says in my head, "Mom?"

In the instant I'm distracted by my human self, a loop is draped over my neck, and I'm caught in the trap. I twist and pull and writhe to get out of it, but it makes the loop tighten more. I don't care! Kill me. I will escape or die.

"Change back or be killed," the woman says.

Something inside me forces my obedience. I want to resist. I want to fight back. I want to stay a wolf, fight as a wolf, die a wolf.

But I can't stop. The wind and the clouds are driven back. The moon goes dark, and I'm human again. I spit blood out on the floor and pull the choking loop away from my neck so I can breathe. My clothes are torn and hanging from me, not serving their purpose, but I don't care.

"What is this?" I ask.

Mom walks forward. "This is your destiny, son. The time of the wolves is here. Help us. Join me, like your brother has."

She steps aside, revealing Nic behind her.

I thought I'd smelled him, but had immediately dismissed it and thought maybe it was part of her I smelled. The part of them that's similar.

It can't be. It makes no sense. Nic isn't even a werewolf. But he is now. I can tell. I smell the werewolf blood in him. But Nic was the good one. Nic was the one in control.

Three remain. But there were five, I was sure of it. Where did the other werewolves go?

"Why?" I ask, my voice pleading.

"Because it is the way of the world, Ben. It is who we are. It is who you are. Sam, too."

I look around the room, frantically searching for Sam, but he's not there. I deflate as I realize I'd called Nic for help. No help is coming. Becca is outside. The fire is burning. Someone will see and call for help. I know that. But I also know it will be too late.

"Becca?" I ask, not wanting the answer.

As though on cue, the another werewolf drags her limp body into the room and drops it carelessly on the floor like she's a bag of trash.

"I told you to stay away from her," Nic says.

"She's fine," Mom says with a smirk.

"What have you done to her?" I roar. I lunge forward, but a werewolf still holds me in the noose. I lash out at him as though I still have claws.

He jumps back and laughs.

"Enough," Nic says to him. "Let him go. He can't take us all on."

Betrayal. It's sharper than any tooth or claw or blade. I'm weakened by it. The henchman takes the loop off me and eases away, ready for me to attempt something. I rush to Becca and check her pulse. Her heart still beats.

I want to hear them tell me their master plan, so I can thwart it, but I also need to save the dogs I'd heard barking and whining. I fear that since they've quieted, it may be too late. Then I catch the scent of a wolfhound, and see Morrigan lying behind them all in the kitchen, as limp as Becca. Oh God, no. This can't be happening.

I did this to her, to her dog. I brought this on them. My mother is behind this.

I purse my lips and try to keep my emotions together. I know what this is. This is the erasure of the Connolly Clan. Becca, Morrigan, the wolfhounds in the barn. It was all so easy.

"Where's Mrs. Russell?" I ask, and my voice cracks.

"She's just visiting a sick friend. Hadn't you heard?" Mom says.

I have no idea what that means, but I know it doesn't sound good. My mind races to come up with a plan to stop all of this, but I have no idea what to do.

CHAPTER 31

Becca

God, my head hasn't hurt this much since the morning after I sneaked the whiskey out of Dad's liquor cabinet last year. Did you get the number of that bus? I open my eyes, but it's dark and I'm woozy. I don't remember drinking. Where am I? What time is it?

I rub my head and detect the smell of smoke in the distance, but can't remember anything that happened. I open my eyes wide to let the light from the moon in. It's almost full. I close my eyes hard, then open them. That's how you see faster in the dark. Something about pupils dilating. Okay, I'm on the floor in the living room.

The moon was big and bright. We were setting bait for the werewolves. Did I sleepwalk?

"Becca, wake up." Someone is shaking me.

"Whatisit?" My words are slurry, and I kind of want to go back to sleep. Did we drink when we set up bait? I push the annoying hands away.

"Becca, are you okay?" Maddie moves around to the other side of me.

Then I get it. This isn't a dream. This isn't a drunken bender. The smell of smoke triggers my memory, and I push myself up on my hands, faltering a little. Something is wrong. Maddie's eyes are telling me something is very wrong.

She turns to someone else. "What do we do?"

"Here. Give her some water," a voice says.

Abby? And a glass appears before me. I drink.

Reality is trying to wipe away the haze. Why am I so stoned? Sober up, girl. Get it together. Then I remember.

"Morri!" I call out, but my voice is hoarse and scratchy. "Where'smydog?" I slur.

She should be here. She's always at my side. I can't function very well. Fuck, fuck, fuck, the dogs in the barn.... I shake my head to snap out of the cloud, but pain radiates through my skull.

"Morri, fuck," I mutter.

"Call her," someone says.

I turn to see Ben's brother beside me. It's the kind of annoying one. Sam.

I look at him, frowning.

He points to his temple. "Call her."

I remember what Grandma'd said about bonding, and I go deep within. I remember how I sensed Morri coming at the dance. I felt something about her that night. Her nearness. I can't do it. I don't feel anything. I hope it doesn't mean the worst. I shake my head.

Maddie and Abby offer their arms to me. Kyle is there, too, standing with his hand on his chin and bracing his elbow with the other hand. Always thinking.

I push myself up to stand and look around me. A dead

guy lies in a sticky mass of blood, the front window is shattered, the living room is trashed. I run to the kitchen, slamming my shoulder into the archway on the way, still unsteady, but I feel no pain. A bonus, I guess. I have to see the barn. A small fire truck is there, still aiming its hose at what's left of the barn. Half of it stands, black smoky marks left along the windows.

I clutch at my heart, and I can't breathe. Oh God, the wolfhounds.

No wolfhounds are running in the yard. No shapes, no sounds, no lumbering goofballs who want hugs and pets. Tears pour from my eyes.

"No" comes out a whisper, then I find my voice and scream. "Noooooooo!" The word forms at the depth of my soul and rips through me, threatening to tear my throat and everything I am out of my body with it.

"Becca, wait. It's okay," Maddie says. "We got the dogs out."

I turn to her, my eyes wide. "You did?"

Sam comes up to me and puts a hand on my shoulder. "We got them. They're okay.

I exhale and put my hand to my heart. "I need to see them. Where are they?" I hold on to the counter as I hurry to the back door. I have to get out of this house.

Kyle helps me. "We saw the fire on our way home. We came back, and two cars were speeding out of the driveway."

Maddie finishes. "One of the dogs had jumped out a window, it looks like, and was scratching at the barn door. We got the doors open and got them all out before they were hurt. We called the vet. She lives on the lake. She picked them up and took them to her office to check them out. They inhaled a lot of smoke.

I count off the wolfhounds' names on my fingers and

check and double-check and triple-check that they got them all, especially the puppies.

"They're fine, but Morrigan wasn't with them," Abby says.

The relief I'd just felt dissipates. Where is she? The last I saw she'd run into the house. I glance to the dead guy and the mess in the living room. Something went down here. At least it's not her lying in a pool of blood on the floor.

"Gran? Mom? Wait, where's Ben?" My mind is clearing, slowly. "I've got to find them."

"We called your mom," Maddie says. "We didn't see Ben or your grandmother." She looks to the others, her eyes cringing a little.

"So no wolfhound, no Gran, no Ben... An attempt to wipe out the other wolfhounds. Who would do this?"

They look to one another. I don't expect them to know.

Then Sam says, "Unfortunately, I have a pretty good idea."

Ben

I can't believe this is happening. I have no choice. Do I? Mom agreed to leave Becca, but she has Mrs. Russell and Morrigan in the van with her other henchmen. Nic and I ride in the car with her. They have me snugly between them. Nic gave me some sweats to wear. They know the drill with werewolves and changing. We don't buy expensive clothes. They are expendable, and it's good to have spares stashed away.

But I couldn't give a shit about that. I focus on the fact that Becca is alive. The fire will draw emergency crews, and they'll see the broken windows. They'll get Becca help. Dad will hear about it on the scanners. He'll take care of it. He'll figure it all out. I focus on that to keep from hyperventilating.

"So this is it, then? You think you can just kill off Mrs. Russell and the new slayer's wolfhound and then what?" I goad them.

"You know what," Mom says, eyes forward on the dark highway.

"Why not kill them already? What's with the big convoy?"

Nic sighs. "Are you going to be annoying about this? We should've just left him in the house."

"He'd help her. He'd help the other mutts," she says.

"Why are Mrs. Russell and the wolfhound still alive?" I ask again. They must be keeping them alive for a reason, and then it hits me. As with everything with werewolves, the moon. Lunacy. Everything happens on the full moon. They want the impact and the power. "Ahhh, right. Tomorrow night."

Mom stares forward, but her hands tighten on the steering wheel.

"Why get them a day early?"

"We want to have everything in order for the ritual," she says.

I nod. "Ohhh, yes, of course, there's a ritual." I roll my eyes.

"More of a celebration," Nic interjects.

"Right, a celebration of the furries," I mock.

Nic turns and clutches my throat in one hand. He's stronger than he's been before, though he's never tried to choke me out. "The werewolf is a strong and noble creature. We've hidden in the shadows for too long. It is time to claim what is ours." He releases me.

I cough and rub my throat. "Right, and you've been a werewolf for what, five minutes? I mean you weren't when I saw you yesterday."

He stews next to me, his lips pursed as he stares out the window.

"So this hiding in the shadows for so long has been like a day?" I laugh. I'm not amused really. I'm sickened. "You're an idiot."

He lunges at me again.

"Enough," Mom says. "He's right. Ben should be the one wanting this. He should be the one wanting to usher in this new era."

Nic turns and puts his elbow on the window, looking out. The car slows and turns in. Of course, the high school.

My mind races to come up with a plan. What can I do? How can I save them? How can I reach Becca? I come up empty.

Mom pulls around to the back of the school, where a lot of the construction trucks and scraps from the rebuild are stacked. Then she drags me out of the car by my arm, her grip supernaturally strong, and hauls me into the building and down where I'm not even shocked to go. The boiler room in the basement.

CHAPTER 32

Becca

Things fall into place very quickly. My mind clears, and I take steps to get them back—Morrigan, Gran, and Ben. The absence of Morri, who I took for granted always being by my side, is greater than I imagined. I feel off. I feel empty. I feel weak, and I hate feeling weak.

And Ben. I long for him. I fear for him, too, but Sam fills us in.

"Our mother is a werewolf. She left us after Ben was born. Or Dad left her, more like. Dad has kept tabs on her as much as possible. Word is, she and her pack are trying to usher in the age of the wolf." He says it all very plainly.

I can't even begin to process this, but it starts to fall into place. Grandma thought there was a werewolf in that house. I thought that was later though. "Wait. Your mother is a werewolf?"

Sam nods and looks away. I feel like there's more to this story, but there's no time to pry for it now. Ben's mother could be what Gran always sensed over at their property though.

"So your mother's pack is trying to usher in this wolf age thing?" I ask.

He nods.

"How does that work?" Kyle asks, pushing his glasses up to the bridge of his nose.

Sam takes a deep breath. "I don't know the details, but the pack will need to get together, make a sacrifice, and probably do some sort of full moon rite." He eyes me carefully as he says this. "The death of a slayer or a wolfhound would probably work. And killing the remaining dogs that might one day become or breed another were-wolfhound was most likely their being thorough."

A sacrifice. Grandma is a slayer until death. And Morrigan of course.

"Tomorrow night?" I ask.

"When the moon is fullest," he says.

I take out my phone and load up my moon phases app. I read all the books and things Grandma wanted me to, but I also got techy, too. There was an app for that.

I check the current moon phase and swipe to tomorrow. "The moon will be at its fullest tomorrow at 11:11 p.m."

"We have less than twenty-four hours," Maddie says, as if I didn't know that already.

I stop talking and start thinking, my mind spinning. I walk outside and go to the barn. The firefighters are rolling up their hoses. The barn is a smoldering mess of wet ash and wood now. I head toward it.

"Whoa there, young lady," a man says, holding his hand out. "It's not safe.

"No shit," I say and keep going. I've come to find that if

you keep on walking, people aren't that likely to confront and stop you. I guess I saw that with Grandma at the murder site.

My friends walk behind me. Sam stops and talks to the firefighter for a few minutes, while I head in.

I walk slowly, like I'm in a haunted house and something might jump out at me, but I'm not afraid. I'm worried. Those poor wolfhounds. Smoke still permeates the room. I see a few stray doggy squeak toys, and my heart breaks for what almost was, and it aches for Morri. I am confident she's still alive…until tomorrow night anyway.

I head to the ladder going up to the loft. The roof is burned away, but the loft is still there. Up I go. Someone calls from outside, but Sam blocks him. I have to get the weapons. I open the cabinet and start taking things out and tossing them down to the first floor in the hay. Swords, daggers, long bows. More carefully with the pistols, a rifle, a shotgun. And very carefully with the Uzi.

"Becca?" Kyle says from below. "What are we going to do with all of this?"

I walk to the edge of the loft and look down. "Ever hear the phrase 'going in with guns blazing'?"

"Yeah."

"Grab a gun."

After some time getting organized and distributing weapons, Mom arrives, frantic. She checks me over and gets the story of what happened from Maddie. I can't talk. I can't think. The police are now on the scene getting statements.

Sam has already called his dad, and he's on the case. Mom goes to deal with the sheriff and chief firefighter. That leaves me free to find our resident witch, aka my drama teacher, Ms. Eden.

Kyle takes that task on. Within a few minutes of him searching on his iPad, he's found an address. "Why do you need a drama teacher for this?"

I was sworn to secrecy, but these people are helping me and know my secret and the whole werewolf thing. I still don't want to out her though. "She can help us. She knows things."

That seems to keep them from asking more questions. Abby drives me, Kyle, and Maddie there, while Sam stays back to help his dad.

It's a small Tudor home with beautiful landscaping in the front, and the hints of a gorgeous garden tease from among the wrought iron fencing that holds it back. I head to the door, hating to wake her at this time of night, but as I step up to the porch, the door opens as though she were expecting me.

"Come in," she says, standing aside and inviting me in. I wave to my friends in the car and hold up a finger.

The inside of the home looks like a mini museum. A Persian rug lies across the floor, paintings in ornate frames hang on the walls, and vases, pottery, and metal sculptures are placed on end tables and bookshelves. Candles and books are scattered throughout. A sturdy, wooden coffee table holds a crystal ball the size of a baseball on top of it. It perches on a stand made of three serpents whose heads hold the orb. A comfortable-looking, overstuffed couch with soft blankets is in the center of the room.

She sits. "You are ready?"

"Tomorrow night," I tell her.

"Where?"

"I'm not sure yet," I say.

She smiles and looks away.

I frown. "What?"

"You will know, and I will find you."

A text from Sam vibrates my phone. It reads, *Dad's working on it, but nothing yet.*

"The ingredients?"

"I think I am a sister of the moon," I tell her.

"I know this," she says.

I'm not sure how. I don't really know 100 percent. It's just a theory, but okay. "There was a dead werewolf at my house. We have some of his blood."

She shakes her head. "No. The werewolf must be alive when you take its blood."

I exhale and slump my shoulders. "I don't know what to do, then. Some werewolves will be there."

She smiles a knowing, motherly smile at me. "It will be fine."

She knows stuff. I don't know how, and I don't know what, but I'll go with that.

"I will be there," she says.

"Where?" She confuses the hell out of me.

"Where you will need me."

"Okay." I turn to leave.

"You do not have to kill them," she says. "The spell will take care of it."

I shrug. "They have my dog and my grandmother. At this point, the spell is a backup plan."

"When living things die, there is pain. Even if you do not particularly care about those who die, but especially if you do."

Okay whack job. I'm starting to feel the same way my grandmother does. It's time to kill them all. They're fucking with the wrong girl now.

I give her a little wave. "Okay, thanks."

"It is okay to care about others. It does not make you weak," she says again.

"Right." What is her deal?

"When we hurt, it means we live."

"Yeah, okay then. I'll see you tomorrow night." I exit as fast as I can. Weirdo.

Our next stop is to the vet's office. Maddie calls Kelly Cole because, of course, she knows her. She stops in at Lake Pizza all the time. She's still there examining them when we arrive.

The office is small, but now totally packed with Irish wolfhounds. Kelly lets us back behind the desk into the kennel room. They aren't in kennels though.

"They really didn't like having the doors shut on them, so I left them open. They're fine." She's lain some dog beds on the floor. The puppies are all in a kennel with the door open. The other wolfhounds have draped themselves around on the various beds.

"The puppies are fine," she says.

I let out a sigh of relief.

Rhiannon and Angus lie outside the kennel with the puppies. They wag their tails and come to nudge me when I walk over.

"Those two are fine. This one here" — she gestures over to Meriden — "I've treated for some minor burns."

I go over and give her a pat. She's an old dog, like Lugh. She lifts her head to lick me, and her tail starts to beat the floor. Her hair is scorched in a few places.

"And her paws were injured a little too. Probably trying to escape the barn." Kelly cringes. "I've given all of them some antibiotics just to be safe, and an anti-inflammatory to make sure there is no internal swelling."

I glance over at Lugh. He's on a blanket but doesn't acknowledge me like the others.

"This one, however, had the worst of it." She goes over and kneels next to him. "He was hacking a lot and having trouble breathing initially, but I've sedated him, and he's calmed down. He really wanted to get out of here."

"What do you mean?"

"We meant to mention that to you," Abby interjects. "He'd jumped through the barn windows and was clawing to get the others out of the barn. Once we got the puppies out, he ran into the house in a panic."

"This is Lugh. He's Gran's—" I start to say were-wolfhound, but realize we aren't alone, so I stop there. "He was probably trying to find her." I stroke his neck. "Poor guy."

"Lugh?" Kelly writes his name down. "Yeah, so I've treated his injuries from the window and from clawing at the door. His paws were pretty bloodied, too, and he has a few bad cuts around his face."

He's really too old for this slaying business but just wanted to protect Grandma, most likely.

"He'll be okay. He just needs rest. But it was a nightmare getting him into my truck. He didn't want to leave the house. And once I got him here, he did everything he could to get back outside, even though he was hurt."

A light bulb goes off, and I turn to my friends. "He's still drawn to her. He can find them. He can lead us to Gran."

Ben

They drag me to the basement of the high school and tie me to a crappy metal office chair. We aren't in the boiler room. It's probably still demolished. This section is old and crummy.

I see about fifty different people through the doorway walking around, all werewolves in human form. I can smell the werewolf blood in them. Unfortunately, Nic is now one of them. Most of them are men, but a few women, like my mom, are in and out. They are setting up a larger room for the ritual. They draw some rudimentary runes and mark on the floor with paint sticks we use to write on car windows to decorate for football games. Who know those things had so many uses?

They are careful not to let me see where Becca's grandmother and wolfhound are. I'm watching constantly for a clue, and listening for someone to make a comment about them or where they are. And I'm using scent to track them. I'm getting absolutely nothing to lead me to them.

Not that I could do anything, tied to a chair like this, but once I know where they are, I'll worry about the ropes around my wrists and ankles.

Mom and her pack aren't hurting me, though they do eye me with disdain. Nic avoids me entirely now. I still can't believe Nic, mature Nic, sensible Nic.

"Why, Nic? Why are you doing this?"

He walks by me like I don't exist. Mom busies herself in the larger room adjacent to mine. I frantically try to come up with something I can do. I'm not used to being so helpless. I'm a good hunter. I'm a good tracker. I can fight with the best of them, and until Nic turned, I could probably beat him. Sam was the best fighter of the three of us. Sam fights without hesitation and without care. Sam fights with emotion. He accepts his wolf side. I've always felt nothing but guilt and shame.

I hate being different. I hate what my mother is. I just want to be a kid. I hate having to worry and fight and struggle against the pull of the moon and the blood. Sam rides through it. He accepts it. He uses it as a strength. But he's not here. And even though he's accepted his wolf side, I know he'd never be a part of this. He knows the wolf thing is for him, and that it's not for everyone. Though I have to question what I think I know. I never would have seen Nic turning on us...by turning.

Nic was always the reasonable one. Nic was the one who kept us grounded. Nic worked the closest with Dad. I don't understand why he'd turn.

"You're an asshole," I tell him as he passes me.

He shrugs.

"After all you've seen me struggle with? Sam? The changes, so painful at first. The pull of the moon, the burning of our blood? Why would you even consider—"

"You always took it for granted. You never appreciated the gift."

"Gift? Are you freaking kidding me? I've fought this since I was a kid."

"You're a fool, then. It made you stronger. It made you faster. You were lucky. You were born with it, but Mom chose Sam—"

"Oh my God, Nic! Are you insane? He happened to be standing next to her. Mom didn't choose Sam to bestow some wonder gift upon him. She chose him to get to Dad, to hurt Dad. We were a mere convenience. You were huddled next to Dad at the time. She just couldn't reach you."

"Still, you and Sam are better fighters, better trackers, better hunters. Better at everything," he spits.

"So this is a sibling rivalry thing? You'd give up your life as a human to turn? To fight the pull? Because you're jealous?"

"I'm not going to fight. I'm going to let it take me over, like them." He points to the larger room.

"Mom's pack? You want to be a dog like them?"

Nic strikes me. A full punch across the jaw. He's never hit me before. It hurts like hell, but I laugh it off and turn back to him.

"I know that feeling," I say and spit blood on the floor. "It's hot, isn't it? Your blood is fire in your veins."

He shakes his fist out and rubs his hands up and down his forearms. His eyes are wide, nervous, darting around. He can feel it, and it scares him, like it did me.

"It's not a good feeling. I know, and it's taken me years to deal with it, and I'm only half werewolf. Nic, you've let them infect you with a disease."

"Shut up!" he roars. "It's too late now. And once the werewolves rise—"

I burst out laughing. "The werewolves rise? You're ridiculous. What, the world will be all running wild, killing, screwing? Is that what you imagine it will be like when the wolves are in charge and give in to their wolf sides?"

"The Alpha said—"

This is a new one on me. "The Alpha? Oh ho, wow. Mom got you in with her Alpha. That's rich. You have the ear of the Alpha. You've been a werewolf for a day. The Alpha doesn't give two shits about you, Nic."

He quiets at that.

"Where is this Alpha?" I'm thinking I can get some information that might help stop this.

"That's enough, Nic," Mom says, coming into the room. "See to the prisoners."

He turns to go.

"That's right, Nic. Obey your mommy like a good lap dog."

He pauses in the doorway before leaving. I laugh and sneer at my mother.

"Watch your tongue," she says to me.

"Oh, Mother dear, you can try to command me, but I will not submit to you."

"Even so. It's too bad you don't want to be a part of the new world. It won't come quickly. There will be fighting and uprisings. Once the slayers are wiped out, and the hounds are extinct, others will fight, we know. Normal people will oppose us, but they will fall. They don't have the strength we have."

"You mean they don't have the strength the slayers have. The Connolly Clan."

"You should choose the winning side, like your brother has," she says.

"I've fought the burning of my blood and the pull of the moon. I've become strong because of my own willpower and determination and stubbornness. Not because of the lycanthropy. If you think for one second I'd give up what I've achieved, what I've worked for on my own, you're nuts. I won't be a slave to the disease, like Nic has chosen. Like you have."

"No?" she asks, and I don't like the confidence in her tone.

I shake my head.

"For the girl?"

God, please tell me they don't have Becca. I don't respond. I stare straight ahead and tap into my meditation. It's taking everything in me not to snap. I set my jaw and stare at the cinder block wall across the room.

"What about for your brother Sam?"

I try not to react.

"Or your father, perhaps?"

I do all I can to keep my heart from speeding up and my blood from burning, but she can sense it, I'm sure.

She smirks at me and pats my head like she's patting a dog, and I jerk away from her touch. "Oh, honey. If I want you to do something, you'll do it. Like a good boy."

CHAPTER 33

Becca

We manage to talk the vet into letting us take Lugh home after she's finished his treatment for the night. She suspects the effects of the sedative will wear off after a few hours. It's been a long night, and the sun is starting to rise.

Lugh sleeps a lot. He normally does, but with his injuries and drugs, he's sleeping more than usual.

"Are you sure you should use him?" Maddie asks.

"I'm not going to fight with him. He's just going to lead us there," I tell her. It's strange taking Lugh and not Morri. My heart tightens and my throat clenches thinking of what she might be going through.

"He's so old and sweet." She pets him while he lies on one of the several dog beds in the living room.

Mom is home, sweeping up the front room. Ben's dad and Sam helped put up a plastic sheet over the front windows for a temporary fix. His dad is going to fix it tomorrow. The sheriff took the dead body. Not surprising,

Mom's jumpy and keeps rubbing the back of her neck. Her brows are knit together.

I walk up behind her and put my hands on her shoulders. "Get some rest."

She laughs. "Me? What about you?"

"I will."

"I know what you're going to do. You're going to try to get them back. Tonight. Don't do it Becca," she pleads.

"Mom, I have to. It's Gran and Morri."

"Morrigan is just a goddamned dog, Becca!" A cry erupts from her, and the sobbing begins. "You are more important."

"Than Gran?"

"Yes! Yes, more important than all of it to me. Mom wouldn't want you to risk your life for her."

"It's what she's trained me for. To fight the monsters."

"That's what she always wanted, to fight the monsters. All of them. Even Dad." She wipes her eyes. "I think I will lie down for a bit. And if you're going to go through with this, you should lie down, too." She goes to her room.

Sam knocks on the front door then comes on in. "I think we've done everything we can do."

I nod and look at my friends who have been with me all night. "You don't have to do this."

"Are you kidding me? I wouldn't miss it for the world," Maddie says.

Kyle and Abby look to each other and nod.

"You could get hurt." My glance drifts over to Lugh. "You could die. You haven't been trained like Sam and I have."

"She's right," Sam agrees.

"We'll play getaway driver, then," Abby says. "We'll be nearby if needed."

"And who says we haven't been trained?" Kyle takes a rifle I'd given him, loads, and locks it in a smooth motion. "I told you, my uncles made me hunt and go to the shooting range and do all sorts of macho bullshit. I may be an honor roll student nerd at school, but I can shoot a bottle of Budweiser off a fence post at 200 yards every time."

We stare at him. My mouth hangs open.

Abby looks him up and down. "That's hot."

"Yeah?" he asks and straightens up a bit taller.

"Very yeah," she says.

I think she may be drooling a little.

"Anyway," I say to get them back on track. "I can't make you do anything. If I could, I'd make you stay back. But if you are going to go, you should rest up. Tonight is going to be a long night."

Or a very short one.

Ben

Nic is an idiot. I saw which way he went when Mom told him to check on the prisoners. He didn't even think to shut the door.

I shake my head and sigh. It's going to be bad. I know it's going to be bad. If Becca gets here, the new slayer... I don't even know what to think. Dad had warned us of the Connollys and slayers in general. From everything he said, they are bad news to werewolves. And if she's a sister of the moon? She could very easily wipe out every werewolf here. With her were-wolfhound, that is. Without Morrigan? And with her crossbow trigger hand still hurt, I hate to think what might happen.

That is, if she even knows where we are. I'd told her my theory about the school basement. I'd told Dad and Sam, too. I hope they remember. I don't know. They're probably still scouring the forest.

If help doesn't arrive, Becca's grandmother and her wolfhound will be killed. That will tear her up. That would tear anyone up, but Becca.... She acts tough, but she cares for both of them deeply. She'll blame herself. She'll never get over it.

I hope she can find us and perform the spell. Wiping out this particular pack whose goal is to kill off the Connolly Clan would make a statement. It would make the other packs afraid and potentially lurk back into hiding. It would make it clear that slayers and wolfhounds are here to stay.

I have to get free. Now that I'm alone, I start working my binds. I have to help Becca save the world.

CHAPTER 34

Becca

The others head home and do whatever they need to do to prepare. And I mainly wait for Lugh to wake up. When he does, I give him water and a steak Gran had in the fridge saved for him. He drinks a lot. The vet said he'd be thirsty. But he only sniffs the steak.

I pat his head. "I'm sorry you got hurt."

He licks at my hand and stands taller, then takes a few loping steps toward the back dog door.

I head him off. "Not yet, big guy. We have to wait a bit longer."

It's all I can do to hold him for the next hour. I end up having to leash him and keep him with me. All he wants to do is take off. He howls and whimpers like I've never heard him before. I take it as a good sign. Grandma must still be alive since he wants to get to her, since he wants to protect her.

I carb up on some leftover pasta before leaving. At this point, I'm jacked and ready to go. My slayer instincts are twitching, and I really want to punch someone like I did that Teddy guy at Lake Pizza.

Soon, but not soon enough, the others arrive, all stocked and ready to go.

"To be honest, I don't know how this is going to work," I tell them. "If I let him go, he'll just take off."

"Ah, I can help you there," Sam says. He takes out a small device about the size of a large paper clamp and clips it on Lugh's collar. "GPS. We use it to track when we hunt."

"Okay, then."

We get in Kyle's car, and Sam drives separately. When they're ready, with Lugh pulling at the leash raring to go, I unclip the lead.

He's off like a barrel racer at the state fair. He dashes down the road, and we follow for half a kilometer or so before he turns into the Mark Twain National Forest.

"No surprise there," I say.

Sam is in front of us and pulls over by the side of the road. He leans out of the driver's window. "I'm watching him on my phone. He's cutting straight through."

"Straight through?"

He watches his phone for a few minutes. "He's running the path to Park High."

Then I remember what Ben had said about the high school and everything that went on there and how he had a theory about where the werewolves might go.

"He's running to the high school. Ben thought they'd hole up there," Sam says, confirming my thoughts. "Let's drive and beat Lugh to it. We can stop him before he gets into trouble. Let's park by the junior high behind the building and walk down to the high school."

We get there way ahead of Lugh. Sam keeps watching

on his phone for Lugh's location in case it happens to change.

"We should go stealthy," Sam says. "Sneak in, see what's going on. I'm not sure what good your crossbow will do at close range."

"Don't worry. I came prepared." I pull aside my denim jacket to reveal a knife at my hip.

Abby, Maddie, and Kyle stay up on the hill. Kyle thought ahead and brought binoculars, and he sets the assault rifle up on a stand that he brought from home, aiming it at the school.

"I can shoot anyone who comes out," he says. "Problem is, I'll only know a werewolf if it comes out a werewolf."

"Just shoot wolves," I tell him.

Headlights flash behind us, and I see another car drive up.

"Crap," I say under my breath.

It pulls in beside us and out steps Ms. Eden. "Hello," she says. "This should be fine."

"How did you... Never mind," I say. "Okay, should you get ready?"

"I am ready. Do you have all of the ingredients?" she asks.

"I don't. I haven't gotten them," I say, and my heart starts to pound. This isn't going to work.

"You have the moon part. Ben has the wolf part," she says.

"He does? And how do you know?" This woman is cray.

"I just know," she says.

"Okay, so how do I get them to you during the spell?"

"Have the ingredients close to the wolves. I do not need to have it. As long as the two are within range and mix while I cast, the spell will work."

"Don't you need to light candles or draw some weird symbols everywhere? Burn some incense?"

"I am fine. You go ahead. Find Ben," she tells me.

I shake my head and shrug. "Okay, guys. Wish us luck." I take a step away.

Maddie jumps up and hugs me. "Good luck."

I awkwardly hug her back. I'm not a big hugger.

"Good luck," Abby echoes.

Kyle gives a casual salute and nods my way.

"You, too, Sam," Maddie says, throwing herself at Ben's brother.

"You good?" Sam asks, looking at me over her head.

"As I'll ever be."

"Then let's do this. LEEERRROOOYYY Jennnnkinnns!" he blurts out, then laughs at his own joke.

We start trodding down the path to the high school, when we see Lugh burst out of the tree line.

"Oh, for fuck's sake!" I say. "I thought you were watching!"

"Crap. I got distracted. There goes stealthy," Sam says. "Text my dad and tell him where we are!" He tosses his cell phone to Maddie who catches it deftly, and he and I bust our asses to get down to the school before Lugh arrives.

Ben

I get my hands free, but I can't bend down to work on my feet. Too many werewolves around. But...if I change...

To change into werewolf form is painful but relatively quick. My paws would slip from my binds, and I'd have a surge of speed, strength, and predatory instinct. There are too many others around who could change just as easily, so I have no delusion that I'll be able to fight them all and save Becca's grandmother and her wolfhound, but I could probably escape and create a diversion. Maybe take out one or two. There are so many. And Becca has only fought the two at the dance before. She nearly died, and then she had me and Morrigan. She's not ready. She's going to need me.

I feel the moon in my blood. It's almost full. At the full moon, during lunacy, my blood runs so hot it almost feels cold, and rushes through my veins. I close my eyes and calm the effect, like I've done my whole life. I'm used to this. I'm good at this now, but I still hate it.

I can feel the moon even though it's not on me. A headache is creeping up the back of my neck. I didn't take my anti-anxiety meds, either, having been captured and dragged here.

A nervous energy runs through the pack in the large room next to mine. At first, I mistake it for the full moon, but I realize it's different. I perk up and use my senses to detail the scene. My sight, my hearing, my sense of smell. Someone else has arrived. Then barks erupt from the basement. I know those to be Morrigan's and am relieved to hear her up and conscious. Then another set echoes hers. Another wolfhound?

Gunshots crack through the relative silence. One, two... That's a 9mm. That's Sam's gun of choice. The others start running and shouting orders.

Mom yells, "Bring them in here, now!"

The others are distracted enough for me to untie my

ankles. No shifting necessary. Things are about to get real chaotic, real quick.

Becca

Lugh beats us to the door and manages to get in. The idiots had left the back door slightly propped open with a wooden triangle doorstop. Lugh sticks his nose in and pushes, with Sam and me running in from behind.

I don't like the odds. This could be a trap or an ambush. There's no scoping it out. Wolfhounds kill first, ask questions later. Lugh starts before we are ready, so it's go time. I switch to instinct mode. Run in. Fight. Get Grandma, Ben, and Morri out. Hope the drama teacher's spell works. Retreat. Hide. Move to Canada. Whatever it takes.

Lugh runs into the building down the hall by the theater, then scratches at a closed door. He's barking and whimpering so much, Sam's index finger at his lips to signal me to go in quietly is in vain.

He shrugs his shoulders and shakes his head. "You ready?" He holds a pistol in each hand.

I load a bolt and take the long knife in my left hand, which also balances my crossbow. I laugh. "Not particularly, but go."

"Should you tie him up?" Sam asks, jutting a chin to Lugh.

"I don't think we can hold him. Let's just go." There isn't time. We weren't able to catch him and leave him in the truck with the others. I hate it, but I don't feel like I have a choice. Through the windows behind us, I see the moon, a huge plate in the sky, reflecting light all over the football field behind the school. It's time.

Just an f'ing dog. I hate myself.

Sam opens the door, and Lugh rushes in, followed shortly by shouts and other muffled barks from down the stairs to the basement.

"Morri!" I call out, and we run in.

By the time we hit the bottom of the stairs, Lugh has taken out one guy and lunged at the throat of another.

"Good doggy," I say, running in and scanning the hall.

The man lets out a gurgled cry and falls limp next to his buddy. Lugh is off.

Sam picks off a guy as he comes around the corner, and another. I save my bolt until needed and just try to keep up with Lugh. We turn the corner of the gray cinder block hallway, and another guy is running up. Sam takes him out.

"Should I just leave?" I joke.

"Naw, you're good," he says.

Lugh skids down the hallway, reminding me of Morri, who starts barking again. Lugh gets to another closed office door and starts scratching at it.

"Lugh, baby? Is that you?" Grandma says from the other side. Her voice cracks, and I can hear her crying. "What a good boy."

More barks erupt from Morri, drowning out whatever Grandma is saying, but Lugh seems to calm, hearing her voice. He sits and his tail pats the ground.

"Get them out," Sam says. "I'll cover you." He watches the hall as I try the door.

"Locked."

"Of course it is," he says, but still stands watching for anyone coming down the hall. "We don't have much time. Break it down."

"I'm sorry, what? Break down a steel office door?" He's nuts.

"Want me to do it for you, princess?" He smirks at me.

"No!" I take a step back and line up for a big sidekick. I take a breath, channel my energy, and hit the door with the blade of my foot as hard as possible.

To my surprise, the door flies open. Morri rushes toward me, but Grandma is tied.

I give Morri a quick pet. "Good girl, we gotta go." Then I hurry to Gran.

She's been knocked around. Her face is bruised. Her eye is swollen.

"What douchebags! Hitting an old woman like this," I say to Sam. "No offense, Gran."

"Well, your grandmother has taken out a few of their kind in the past. Just saying," Sam says.

I look her over quickly while I cut her ropes. "My God, Gran, your eyes are so big and swollen."

"Don't worry about that, honey. Let's just get out of here."

"What about the pack and Ben?" Sam asks.

"We get Gran and Morri out. That stops the full moon rite thingy. We have to get Gran to safety." I hold out an arm and help her up.

Lugh flanks her, and Morri flanks me. Sam nods at the door and covers our backs. Just as we start down the hallway to leave, movement sounds behind us.

"Not so fast. We weren't quite finished with you yet."

Of course not. It couldn't have been that easy.

Sam pivots quickly, guns leveled at the woman talking. Then he seems to wilt. "Mom?"

"Drop your weapons," she orders.

The wolfhounds start losing their minds. I'm about to let them loose when Nic comes out from the room behind them, holding Ben by the scruff of his hoodie and a knife at Ben's throat.

"Gran, grab Lugh!" I shout, and I take Morri by the collar. "Down, Morri!" I order.

"Lugh, heel!" Grandma tells her were-wolfhound.

The two sit and settle, but I can feel the anxious energy coursing through Morri. They both tremble with excitement, waiting for the bite.

"Nic? What are you doing?" Sam asks, as confused as I am.

Nic releases Ben who answers on his behalf. "He's turned and joined Mom's pack. Isn't that just great?"

Sam frowns and shakes his head.

"What the actual fuck?" I ask. "Your mom and her pack were going to kill Gran and my were-wolfhound!" I say to Nic, as though that should have deterred his joining her.

"*Are* going to," Nic corrects me.

I calculate the odds. I have a strategy in my head and then usually a plan B, C, and what the fuck, abort mission. I shift to plan B, which includes releasing the hounds. They'd do a lot of damage, but someone else could also get hurt.

Then I remember the spell. I have the sister of the moon blood. I need wolf blood. There are two living wolf people right in front of me. I just need their blood. I take my knife to my hand and cut it until I bleed. Morri whimpers and shakes harder.

"Becca, what—" Ben says, then his eyes clear.

I can tell he remembers what we need for the spell. "We seem to be at an impasse," I say.

Ben's mom narrows her eyes at me, watching my hand bleed. She cocks her head, confused. Behind me, people rush down the stairs. Lugh's and Morri's ears twitch. My moonstone necklace is glowing brighter than it ever has.

"Mom, why are you waiting? We have them surrounded. Let's just grab them. She's just a girl." Nic says.

Fuck, I hate when people say that.

"I'm just a girl, with a really big wolfhound," I say, and I let go of Morri's collar.

Ben

I didn't get far before Nic grabbed me. He'd kept his eyes on me pretty closely. Obviously, I was there for bait or leverage. Why else had they kept me? He drags me out and throws me in front of Team Slayer. This is embarrassing. Sam's helping her. On one hand, that's good, because he's an experienced hunter. On the other hand, not so great because he won't be able to kill Mom or Nic. I know I wouldn't.

The wolfhounds are going nuts, and then Becca cuts her hand. Why would she... The spell. Ms. Eden must be out casting the spell now. That means all of these werewolves in the pack will be cured and essentially powerless against slayers and hunters. That means Nic will be cured, Mom...me and Sam. I hadn't thought that through.

I don't care. I don't want to be a werewolf. I'm tired of fighting it. I'm tired of being ashamed and guilty. But

Sam? Sam has embraced it. Does he know about the spell? Does he know what's going to happen if I join my blood with hers?

I have to do something, but I don't know what. All I know is blood will be spilled. I do the only thing I can think of and change.

Becca

Ben shifts into a werewolf right in front of me.

"What the fuck?" I say, but things are happening too quickly for me to process that Ben, my crush, my heart-throbby hunter guy is a werewolf. How is that possible? How did my necklace not glow like crazy all those times I was with him? How did Morri not kill him on sight?

Werewolf Ben turns on his brother Nic. Morri and Lugh run down Mommy Dearest, who takes off through the door into another room. Sam runs up and punches Nic out cold.

I'm the slayer. I can't just stand here with my teeth in my mouth. I gotta go kick some ass and look impressive.

"Gran, stay here," I say.

"You're kidding, right?" She dashes into the room before I do.

Werewolf Ben runs after the others. I take off after him.

A low rumble of thunder shakes the building. A larger reverberation of growls, snaps, and barks echoes inside. I get into the larger room that is decked out for a ritual: candles, runes on the floor, incense, goblets of dark liquid,

240

ritual daggers, the whole deal are all laid out ready for whatever they were planning on doing.

The room is big and open, lined with metal shelves storing maintenance supplies. A thin row of windows lines the wall near the ceiling, and the light of the moon shines down in the middle of the casting circle. I hope Ms. Eden is casting, too. I hope she's had enough time. I've got to get my hands on a wolf's blood, right freaking now.

Pop, pop… Sam is using his pistols.

I grab the first man-wolf I see and punch him, like I did the guy at the pizza place. Owwww, my hand isn't 100 percent yet. Luckily, I've got two of them. I hit him with a left hook. He grabs me, picks me up, and throws me on the ground. Holy fuck, that's painful, but unfortunately for him, it only makes me want to beat his ass more. I get up and sidekick him as if he were a steel office door. He flies backwards into metal shelving and slumps to the ground, gallon cans of paint falling on him for good measure.

Whoa, I got skills. "I got this!" I shout to whoever is listening and run up to the biggest guy there. I want to send a message. I'm getting cocky. I walk up to this big Alcide looking wannabe. His shoulders are back, his chest out, and I swing and punch him as hard as I can in the jaw, just like with the LaRette dude at Lake Pizza. But his face doesn't smush in slow mo. He barely flinches, and my hand hurts again. "I don't got this!" Wolfman draws his hand back to hit me right as werewolf Ben lunges for him, throws him on the ground and goes off again. "Someone's got this."

Morri and Lugh are wreaking havoc beside me. They've ripped out two throats to my one unconscious guy. Grandma has gone for Ben's Mom. She's got her by the neck and is pushing her back up against the wall.

Werewolf Ben has thrown a guy on the ground and goes off again.

I jump on the back of a man who was heading toward Grandma and pull him away. He slams me against the wall, knocking my blade out of my hand. I get him in a choke hold until he falls. I kick him in the face when he's on the ground, then I run for another one.

I punch, I kick, I grab and get punched, kicked, grabbed. Grandma has a ritual dagger up to Ben's mom's throat in the corner. Lugh covers Grandma, keeping everyone else back.

So much blood and so many downed werewolves. We're killing them all. I need to find a dropped man-wolf guy who still lives and use his blood.

Morri is barking behind me.

"Becca, the spell!" Ben shouts.

I turn to see him in the doorway of the room, standing bare-chested and holding his hoodie around his waist. He holds out a bleeding hand towards me. Werewolf blood.

I run to him, reaching for him, hoping the spell works, hoping we can cure this. I take his bloody hand with mine, and he pulls me into him, kissing me. I forget everything around me, which is totally stupid, but this kiss is my entire life. I want to drown in it, die in it, live in it, slay in it.

Glass crashes around me. The cool night autumn wind comes in through the window. My eyes are closed. I'm safe in this kiss. I'll never open my eyes again. I don't want it to end. I want to stop the fighting, stop the pain, stop the clouds in the sky. There is nothing else.

"Stop where you are!" Ben's dad is squatted down, leveling a gun through the window at his estranged wife.

A few other uniformed officers, Kyle, Maddie, and Abby are there looking down at us, too.

The wind whips my hair around and then fades away. The room has quieted, and Ben pulls back.

"Are you okay?" he asks.

I reluctantly open my eyes and look around the room. Half of the man-wolves are standing around, looking puzzled, the other half taken out. Lugh has one by the throat and shakes. Morri runs to me. Grandma threatens Ben's mom with a knife to her throat, and Sam has dropped his weapons and stands stone still, his eyes wide. He puts a hand to his heart, as though feeling for it. He looks around desperately like he's lost his phone or something more important, maybe.

"Hey, Red?" Ben asks me, searching my eyes. "Nice hoodie. You okay?"

I snap out of it and look into his different-colored eyes, realizing I wear his Chiefs hoodie all the time now. "I'm okay. You?"

He nods.

"You're...naked."

He shrugs. "It happens."

"And you're a werewolf."

"Half," he says. "I was going to mention that at some point."

"We'll talk about it later," I tell him.

"Is the spell done?" Grandma asks, without taking her eyes off Ben's mom.

"It's done," Maddie assures her from the window.

"Let's get them out of here, then. Lugh!" She calls off her dog.

The sheriff disappears from the window, and Kyle offers to run to Ben's gym locker for his tracksuit. The wolfhounds stay alert, eyes on the soon-to-be prisoners, and they stay close to us. Grandma isn't giving

Ben's mom any slack whatsoever.

I stare into Ben's eyes like an enormous dork. I'd be embarrassed if he weren't reciprocating, but he is, so it's hard to focus on the task at hand. We're just waiting for the cops to get in here to cuff them anyway at this point.

"I should...uh...get some clothes, I guess," Ben says.

I laugh. "I guess so, if you must."

"Becca Belle Redford," Grandma chastises me.

I blush.

"Ben, why did you do this?" his mom asks as Ben turns to go. "You could have had everything. We could have ruled the pack."

We all look at her at the end of the room, Grandma holding her back. My grandma kinda kicks ass.

"I don't want that, Mom. I'm happy to be done with it."

"Ben, you could have become the Alpha," she tells him.

"Where is the Alpha?" Grandma asks, pushing the knife into Ben's mom's neck.

Something isn't right. I have a strange feeling. Every time Ben turns to dismiss his mom, she calls out to him to draw his attention. Morri's ears flick back, and Lugh's follow suit. It's too late that I realize she was distracting us all.

"You little son of a bitch!" Nic roars, staggering into the room holding his injured jaw. He levels a gun at Ben.

Sam, who is closest to the door, lunges for him, but no longer has his preternatural speed. Morri darts over to take him down. We all turn to look at Nic. It's reflex. And in that moment it takes to get us all focused on Nic, even Grandma, Ben's mom hits Gran's knife-wielding forearm, knocking the weapon loose. She draws a blade from her own waistband and strikes for Grandma.

Grandma dodges and stumbles backwards, falling to the ground. Ben's mom is lightning fast, even without her werewolf powers. She's on top of Grandma, straddling her before I can take a step in their direction to get to them.

"Gran!" I scream.

Ben's mom raises the knife and is about to plunge Grandma straight in the chest when Lugh leaps in for a bite. With a yelp, he grabs her neck and knocks her down.

I rush to Gran's side. "Are you okay?"

"Yes, yes." She waves me away. "Lugh!" she says, reaching for him.

My instinct snaps me to, and with Morri at my side, I jump on Ben's mom who is still conscious. I give her a good crack across the jaw, and she's out like mom after a bottle of wine. I turn to see Sam and Ben have Nic on his stomach on the floor, hands behind his back, his gun across the floor.

And next to me, Grandma is cradling a lifeless Lugh, tears running down her cheeks, the knife protruding from his chest.

CHAPTER 35

Ben

See, the thing is, I don't feel any different. The full moon still pulls at me. I have a headache still too. Maybe it was kissing Becca, and that's messing with my mind. Maybe I just don't feel the spell, but Sam and Nic seem to feel a noticeable difference.

"How could you take that from me?" Nic glares at me. "Finally, I was going to be something, be someone."

The officers drag him away in cuffs.

I go to the office they'd had me tied up in and put on clothes Kyle got for me, while they are carting away the others. They still have to interrogate them about the murders. They still have to prove it was them. Though we hunters know, the law has to operate within its own parameters.

I dress then stand in the door as they drag Mom away. She looks back at me, and her eyes actually seem sad. I'm sure mine only seem cold and detached. It's what I feel, anyway.

Becca comforts her grandmother, still on the floor with her were-wolfhound, holding him, rocking him, and crying. Becca apologizes over and over, while Morrigan whimpers and paws at Becca, as though trying to comfort her.

Sam's eyes are glazed over. He's in shock, and Dad pats him on the back while he watches as they take Mom down the hall. He hides his emotions pretty well.

I go over to Becca and put a hand on her shoulder. "Hey, Becca. I'm sorry."

She looks up at me and shakes her head. Her mouth is twisted down, holding in a cry. Her eyes are filled with tears.

"Oh, sonny," her grandmother says, wiping away the tears. "It's not your fault." She gently lays Lugh's head on the floor and eases the dagger out of his chest.

Morrigan comes over and sniffs at him, whining some more. Mrs. Russell pushes herself up, and I help them both up.

"The life of a were-wolfhound is longer than most, but not infinite. He died doing what he wanted to do. He died protecting me. That's what Lugh lived for," she says, her voice choking on that last line.

"I'll bring him home for you," I tell her. "We can bury him in your yard if you want. I can help. Whatever you want." I feel like complete crap.

She nods and purses her lips. "Thank you, Ben. That would be nice. I have a spot for him."

Becca looks at me. "Thank you. I'm going to get her home."

"Yeah, sure," I say.

I want to kiss her. I want to finish what we started. I want to hold her, but now isn't my time. She's a slayer. She has to deal with her family. The two of them leave.

Morrigan stays behind and sniffs at me for a minute, then looks right at me. It's unnerving to say the least. She doesn't growl, but she doesn't lick my hand or wag her tail either. She stares as though trying to tell me something. Becca gives a sharp whistle, and after another second or two, Morrigan takes off down the hall after her slayer.

"Ben?" Dad snaps me out of it. "Let's go."

Becca

It's a difficult night. Grandma takes the death of Lugh as well as can be expected, and it's hard on her. Kyle drives us home, and I get her some tea, then help her get ready for bed. She refuses to go until Ben and Sam bring Lugh's body to us.

"They're here, Gran. You can go now," I say.

She staggers over to the window and looks out to make sure, then nods and goes to her room.

I walk outside to greet them. Ben gets out of the truck and opens the tailgate.

"Thanks for doing this," I say.

"Of course, Becca." He leans against the truck. "I'd do anything…"

The moon is still bright but has dipped down behind the trees by this point. A cool breeze blows, and I pull his Chiefs hoodie around me.

"I never gave this back."

He smiles. "Looks better on you."

Swoonsville.

"Go inside. We'll take care of this," he tells me.

"No, I can help."

He takes two shovels out of the back. "Do you know where she wanted him?"

I nod. "Over here." I lead them behind the barn where a row of large stones lines the barn.

Each one has a Celtic cross and a name engraved in it. Brigid, Lir, other past wolfhounds I never met. He and Sam put the shovels to the earth, and I go into the barn to find a third to help them. A lump forms in my throat, and I do all I can to keep from crying in front of them.

CHAPTER 36

Becca

Ben, Sam, and Ben's dad, Ryan, spend the next few weeks rebuilding the barn. Grandma gives them a few new specifications to add to update it: one, of course, being a new weapons cabinet and training area upstairs, complete with speed bags, weights, punching bags, and dummies for practice.

Mom seems to spend a lot more time at home when Ryan's dad is working on the barn. The divorce papers arrived last week, but she only just told me. I give her a look.

"What?" she asks as she comes out with her second carafe of coffee for him.

"Nothing. He's hot," I tell her.

Her eyes widen. I smirk at her.

"Becca Belle Redford!" Her face turns red.

"Go for it, Mom. Just don't get married because I don't want to date my stepbrother. That'd be gross."

She rolls her eyes at me and goes to hit on Ryan.

Grandma comes outside to watch, using a cane. She got pretty banged up in the fight, but she's tough. A trail of wolfhounds follows her out. We got them from the vet last week, and they all seem fine. The puppies are starting to get more and more rambunctious. Gran seems quieter now, though. Empty maybe, without her dog.

I've been working on slayer training, but more specifically sister of the moon training. Ms. Eden sent me a book on it, one that Grandma hadn't been able to find, but I let her look it over before using it. Something is off about Ms. Eden, and she has access to things Grandma hasn't encountered in her fifty years of slaying. But so far, she's helped us.

One thing I read is that I heal faster and become stronger the brighter the moon is, so most of my injuries clear up within a few days.

If it's possible, Morri sticks more to my side now than ever.

As does Ben. I smile just thinking about him.

Ben

She's amazing. More amazing than I thought at first. More amazing than I thought possible. I hate to finish fixing up the barn. I like being around, and I'm so glad we now have a partnership with Mrs. Russell and that she doesn't hate me anymore.

But I am still half werewolf. I still feel the heat in my blood, and I can still change. The spell didn't affect me.

Though Sam is crushed that he was cured and is spending a great deal of time off on his own when he's not working with Dad.

I don't know how to tell Becca, and unfortunately we haven't had a lot of time alone, but we're back to school in our normal routine again tomorrow. I should ask her out or plan something.

We finish the last of the barn and pack up the truck. Dad spends a lot of time talking to Becca's mom. Not sure how I feel about that, but he deserves to be happy.

I saunter over to Becca when I've put my stuff away. She's sitting on the back steps, smiling at me. "Hey."

"Hey yourself," she says.

"We've finished up everything."

"I see that. Thank you." She stands.

"Soooo, see you at school tomorrow, I guess." I really am terrible at asking her out.

"I guess so." She's smirking at me.

"Okay, then. See ya." I know I just said "see ya," but I don't want to leave. I guess I'm done, and since I don't live here, I kinda have to leave eventually.

I turn and she takes my arm and spins me back around, kissing me. We haven't kissed like this since the full moon, and even without the full moon making me half crazy, I'm still half crazy when she kisses me. It's as if she channels the energy of the moon inside her. It makes me so hot, I feel cold, and I can't pull away. Luckily she does.

"Wow," I say.

"Wow what?" She grins.

"You make me crazy like the full moon. It's like you're my moon." I feel like an idiot. I don't even know what I'm saying anymore.

For whatever reason, though, she kisses me again.

Deeper, longer. Then afterward, she just grins at me. Chicks are weird.

"See ya," she says, and I stand there like an idiot giving her some googly-eyed look.

"Ben, come on!" Dad shouts.

"Wow, yeah. I gotta—"

"Go," she says, smiling.

I turn and jog to the truck, feeling invincible.

Becca

Back to school awesomeness. It's not too bad, actually. Maddie is a burst of perkiness as usual, and I seem to notice Abby hanging around Kyle's locker a few times with an atypical grin on her face, and with Kyle leaning up against it like some sort of cool guy with swagger. That's not normal. It makes me smile though.

Ms. Eden does her drama class as usual, but holds my eye contact a little long once and gives me a knowing look. Yeah, she freaks me out, but seems cool, I guess.

And I get to sit with Ben. "Are you busy after school?" he whispers to me.

Frig. "Uh, yeah, unfortunately. I have detention."

"Again?" he asks, kind of surprised.

"Apparently."

"Why this time? You haven't ditched without me, have you?" Awwww, he seems hurt.

"No, I cussed in MacIntyre's class."

"Oh, yeah, that'd do it."

"Fucking stupid. It's just a word. Or several."

"Okay, then." He lowers his gaze and looks at his hands. Awww, now he seems disappointed.

"Want me to come by later?" I ask.

"Maybe."

The day drags on as it is known to do in high school. No more classes with Ben make it go by even slower. I look for him after school before I head to the detention room, but he's nowhere to be found.

I find detention, and Mr. MacIntyre folds a corner of his newspaper down and eyes me over his glasses. He glances down to a roster. "Rebecca Redford, there you are." He always calls me Rebecca. I hate it.

"Becca," I correct him. For the millionth time.

Five other losers are already sitting down. They turn to look at me.

"You're late," Mr. MacIntyre says.

I almost swear in response at realizing I did, in fact, arrive late, but I hold my tongue. Do not respond. I've come to realize it's best not to confirm nor deny guilt in most situations. I take a few steps in to prevent him from having to say anything else to me. It doesn't.

He gestures to a box on the corner of his desk. "Phone here. Sit down. Study. Don't talk. You're in for an hour and a half today."

As if I weren't clear on this whole process already. It's my fourth detention, and we haven't even hit second term yet.

I drop my phone in the Adidas box already holding five others. A stab pierces my heart. An hour and a half with my phone out of reach? Cruel and unusual. I should probably write a letter to the editor of the student newspaper in the next hour and a half.

I settle in at a desk by the window and take out my geometry homework. Might as well make use of the time. A minute later, I hear a *tink* on the glass next to me. I look outside to see Ben standing by his truck in the parking lot, smiling. He makes a roll-down-the-window motion.

I glance to MacIntyre, who is buried in his newspaper, then turn the crank on the window to open it out. Ben hurries back into his truck and turns on some music. David Bowie's "Heroes" rings out across the parking lot, wafting up to the window. I smile.

Ben walks around his truck, points at me and then at his radio, and shouts up to me. "You're a hero, Red!"

I can't stop smiling. I roll my eyes and shake my head.

Then he holds up a sign that reads: *Will you go to the homecoming dance with me?*

I smile my face off and nod. He gives me a thumbs-up before heading out in his truck.

And I can't get that song out of my head.

Later when I get home, Grandma meets me in the driveway. "Becca, come here. I want to show you something." She takes me into the barn.

"What is it?"

"Sam left his shirt here yesterday."

"Okay, so?"

"So this." She opens the door to the barn, and on the floor is Sam's red and black flannel shirt being ripped to shreds by one of the puppies.

I frown. "I don't get it."

"Beltane is destroying it."

"She's a puppy," I say.

"And he was a werewolf a few weeks ago. It has his scent on it. I think we have another were-wolfhound on our hands." She claps her hands together and holds them up under her chin. The smile on her face is enormous.

I look down at the puppy, my eyes wide. And with that, little Bel turns toward us and runs, her tiny teeth bared to challenge us.

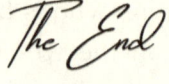

ACKNOWLEDGMENTS

This time special thanks goes to my Other Worlds box set organizer goddesses extraordinaire, Rebecca Hamilton and Monica Corwin. *Becca Redford* first appeared in that box set and with their expertise and the hard ass work of my other set authors, we made the *USA Today* bestseller list. Without those awesome authors working together, we never would have done it. I made some super friends there I can't wait to meet, but from the set I especially want to mention Shawnee Small, my good twin (which makes me the evil twin, but whatever works). She organized the hell out of this set. Also special thanks to LaVerne Thompson Allyson Lindt, Amy Gale, and RA Steffan. This group of eager beaver /cool bitches made it happen with their encouragement, venting, gifs and overall awesomeness. Thanks girls. #forevergrateful

Thanks to Lindsey Loucks at Midnight Library Services for editing this book. Much love to Romkey's Roadies, my rowdy street team. Thanks to a few of my favorite bloggers *Mommy's Late Night Book Up* and *The Two Brains of Book Reviewers*. Thanks to the other box sets out that who swapped with us to share our book! Dionne Lister, you rock! A special gratitude goes to author Cathryn Fox for her generous support, and thanks to my beta readers Amber and Bailey. As always, thanks to my awesome writer peeps from the Romance Writers of Atlantic Canada.

Not that it directly relates to the creation of this book, but thanks to animal rescue everywhere, especially Litters 'n Critters who does awesome work in my area.

And of course, thanks to my amazing readers. I hope you enjoyed the series.

Shawna Romkey

Shawna writes and teaches while living on the shore of Nova Scotia with her husband, two sons, and two goofy dogs (one being a giant, werewolf hunting Irish Wolfhound named Beltane.)

SIGN UP FOR SHAWNA'S NEWSLETTER HERE!
https://landing.mailerlite.com/webforms/landing/r7d7h1

READ MORE FROM SHAWNA ROMKEY
http://ow.ly/E0nV30dF2BR
http://www.shawnaromkey.com/

CONNECT WITH SHAWNA ON SOCIAL MEDIA!
Facebook:
https://www.facebook.com/pages/Shawna-Romkey-Author/137998326331706

Twitter: https://twitter.com/sromkey

Goodreads:
https://www.goodreads.com/author/show/6869437.Shawna_Romkey

Pinterest: https://www.pinterest.com/shawnarp/

Instagram: https://instagram.com/shawna_romkey/

Please review this book on your favorite website, blog or social media outlets, and share it with other readers. Your thoughts matter! Thank you.